Lady Ace

BY

SANDRA FARRIS

iUniverse, Inc.
New York   Bloomington

Lady Ace

iUniverse books may be ordered through booksellers or by contacting:

iUniverse
1663 Liberty Drive
Bloomington, IN 47403
www.iuniverse.com
1-800-Authors (1-800-288-4677)

ISBN: 978-1-4401-1967-5 (pbk)
ISBN: 978-1-4401-1968-2 (ebk)

Library of Congress Control Number: 2009921081

Printed in the United States of America

iUniverse rev. date: 1/21/2009

This book is dedicated to my family, friends, and my newest grandson, Tristan Farris. Also to my hero and long time friend, Linda Griffiths who is valiantly fighting a debilitating battle for her life.

A special thanks to Damon Farris for his help and to Deputy T.E. Koukalik, Special Operations with the Pima County Sheriff's Department.

iUniverse Titles by Sandra Farris

Lady Ace

Wind Dancers (with Darlene McKeen)

Can You Hear the Music?

Acknowledgments

Dennis Farris, my son, for the cover of this book
Darlene McKeen, my sister, for the opening poem
Zaonii Sierra for her expert knowledge of the Spanish
language.
Melinda Islas who bravely edited my manuscript.

Lady Ace

Ever wonder what it would be like to fly?
Well, when I was a little girl so did I.
I'd look at the birds and envy their wings
Flying so high, what joy it must bring!
They seemed so free and without bounds,
Flying above all the worldly sounds.
So it was no surprise when I was grown
I'd chase the paths the birds had flown.
Now I fly with all my felicitous friends
Above it all, where freedom transcends.
Away from my troubles I'm set free
To chase my dreams, my destiny.
Through the clouds I speed with great force.
A destination in mind, I've set my course.
On the ground I'm just another pretty face
But up here I'm known as Lady Ace.

Darlene McKeen

Lady Ace

Prologue

Patrick O' Brien unfolded his six-foot-two frame from the Piper Lance aircraft in which he had been confined the past three hours. He reached toward the sky, stretching lazily, straightening the kinks from his body, then glanced around the small landing field, taking in the tiny antiquated building that displayed a two-tiered sign proclaiming "Office" and "Cafe". Something about this whole scene didn't quite feel right, but he couldn't put a name to it.

Patrick sensed he was being watched, much like in 'Nam when the jungle had eyes. So strong was his feeling he almost climbed right back into the plane to leave. The man he was supposed to meet could be the difference between feast and famine, though. The deal he offered would put a substantial cash flow back into Patrick's charter business, plus some rat-hole money.

There was no one around, neither the man with whom he had been working, nor the financier he came up here to meet. Patrick glanced at his watch. Two o'clock. Two hours to take off and get out of the Colorado mountains before darkness settled in.

Again uneasiness shot fingers of electricity up his spine, causing the fine hair at the back of his neck to stand at attention. Once more his gaze took in the surroundings, revealing nothing out of the ordinary. Perhaps a strong cup of hot coffee would chase away the ghosts.

A bell clinked against the door as Patrick entered the cafe side of the building. He walked to the counter and swung a leg over the stool, settling stiffly on the faded red plastic cushion that sighed and creaked beneath his weight. Dark, eager eyes watched from the back room, an unnatural brightness filling them as the aviator came into view.

Patrick reached for the cup turned upside down on the matching saucer, righting it with a dull clunk of ceramic hitting ceramic. He picked up the laminated menu and scanned its length, glancing up as a man approached from the opposite side of the counter, a coffee pot in his hand.

"*Café, Señor?*" the man asked, his voice barely above a whisper.

Patrick nodded and returned his attention to the menu, looking up again briefly to put cream and sugar into the steaming liquid. Laying the menu aside, he sipped gingerly from the mug. Grimacing slightly, he added more cream and sugar before he was satisfied.

"What can I get for you, Honey?" The gravelly voice belonged to a heavy- set woman with flaming carrot-color hair and watery blue eyes. Patrick guessed her to be around seventy-five. She was wearing a stained, once-white uniform with a multi-colored handkerchief arranged carefully above the left breast. She reeked of cigarette smoke. He smiled at the walking stereotype.

"I was supposed to meet someone here. You haven't seen anyone who looked as though they were waiting for me, have you?"

"Ain't nobody here 'cept me and the cook. Hasn't been nobody but us most of the afternoon."

"Well, maybe I'll have one more cup of coffee while I wait." He glanced over his shoulder and out the window, but no one was there. He turned back to the counter just as the cook came from the back, coffee pot in hand again, and poured more of the brew into Patrick's mug. Silently, the man turned back to the kitchen, taking the pot with him instead of placing it on the coffeemaker's electric burner. *Must be his own private stock.* Patrick smiled to himself.

Patrick waited until the daylight began to drain from the valley. The sun had already dipped halfway behind the mountain, its rays painting pink streaks across the deepening blue skies. The waitress had disappeared into the back and he didn't see the cook anywhere, so he looked at the bill and tossed a handful of coins on the counter. He suddenly felt drowsy as he pushed himself from the stool and wandered out into the crisp, cold air.

In the deepening shadows around his plane he caught a flicker of movement. Someone waited there for him, but he couldn't see who it was. *Must be Mr. Johnson. Good, we can get the hell outta here.*

"You're the cook!" Patrick recognized the man, surprise filling his voice. "What are you doing out here?" He began searching his memory for his high school Spanish.

"I'm the man you have been waiting for."

"You speak English?" Patrick wiped his forehead as though trying to clear his confusion. "Are you Johnson?"

"That'll do for now. Let's get this plane in the air. I'll fill you in as we go." The man chuckled. *An evil sound*, Patrick thought briefly, as they climbed into the aircraft.

Patrick went through his pre-flight checks, ignoring a slight dizziness, attributing it to the Colorado altitude. Once they got airborne they could leave the snow-capped mountains behind and he would be fine.

Johnson picked up a bundle from beneath his feet and unwrapped it as the plane raced down the runway and began its laborious climb.

"Maybe you can fill me in on the details—your partner was a little vague." Patrick spotted the parachute his passenger was putting on and laughed, "You don't need that. I can assure you I know how to handle this plane." An overwhelming vertigo swept over him suddenly and he shook his head to clear it. His vision began to blur. He blinked slowly, trying to see the man seated beside him.

"You don't get it, O'Brien. We're parting company real soon." He stared at Patrick intensely for a moment. "But before I go I want to make sure that mickey I slipped you is working real good."

"Why? Who?" Patrick blinked again and focused with difficulty on his passenger. Something was familiar about the man. When the passenger took off the phony beard and wig, he knew. "You!"

"Yes. Me. And I wanted you to know who murdered you." Johnson grinned and checked out the growing darkness below. He spotted the beacon planted earlier indicating where he should jump and he pushed at the door. "Well, *adios*. This is where I get off." He pushed even harder and jumped through the opening.

Patrick's reflexes seemed to be in slow motion. He turned his attention back to the instrument panel, horror registering in his face—horror in the realization of what was happening to him. Again he shook his head, his concentration and vision waning. Ahead of him a sun-lit peak stood directly in the plane's path, but try as he would Patrick could not summon the strength to pull back on the yoke to rise above it.

He turned his thoughts to his daughter and called out. Kasey's name resounded in the cockpit cabin. He closed his eyes, giving in to the potion draining his consciousness. A tear slipped from his closed lids.

A bright light filled the skies as the plane crashed into the side of the mountain. Like the tree that falls in the forest, the sound of the explosion reached no human ears . . .

Chapter One

San Fernando Valley, California

Kasey O'Brien sat at her desk, an unfolded aeronautical chart and flight plan spread out in front of her, writing figures on the flight plan. She blew a breath upward, causing her blond bangs to billow out while she gave the figures the once over.

When Norm Lang, Cimmaron Air's part-time pilot, came into the office Kasey transferred her attention to him, revealing the shifting emerald lights of her eyes. He walked over to her and checked his watch.

"What time will he be here?"

Kasey glanced toward the parking lot. "He just drove up, and just in time, too. I'm filing the flight plan now."

Alice Greenwood stopped opening the mail, a stern expression on her face. "Don't get too attached to this fellow, Kasey. His genes have worked too hard to make that pretty face and I doubt if they had much energy left to make him good-hearted, too."

Kasey smiled fondly at her secretary. Alice Greenwood, a widow and grandmother, helped out in the office several times a week as needed. "Not to worry, besides he isn't interested in someone like me."

"He should be so lucky," Alice muttered. She shook her head and returned to her job.

Kasey didn't miss the remark. Grinning, she walked over to the wall phone marked FSS USE ONLY-DIRECT LINE and picked it up.

Neal Harrison sauntered through the front door, greeting Alice and Norm. Seeing that Kasey was on the phone he addressed Norm, "How're we doing on time?" He walked over and set his bag down by the hangar door.

Norm pointed to Kasey. "She's filing now and the Baron's ready. Here, I'll take that." He picked up Neal's bag and went into the hangar.

"How's it going, Kasey?"

Kasey held up a wait-a-moment pen to Neal, then wrote on a pad. After the report was filed she went outside and walked around inspecting the two-engine plane. Neal was right behind her. She checked the right engine oil then stooped under the wing and drained fuel into a small clear plastic cup. Since water forms from condensation and settles at the bottom of the fuel tank, she wanted to make sure there was no water or contaminants there.

When everything met with her approval, Kasey swiftly boarded the plane and began checking out the instrument panel. After putting Neal's luggage in the hatch, Norm climbed up on the opposite side of the plane, his knees resting on the wing and his upper body inside the cockpit. He cleaned all the windows on his side and then handed the cleaner to Kasey to clean hers. He jumped down and stood behind the left engine, talking to Kasey through a small opening in the window. Neal struggled aboard, stepping on the wing then folding himself into the front seat beside Kasey.

"I'll give you a call when I get there. I want to be back early this evening. When Josh gets back tell him I'll see him first thing in the morning and that Victor will be here a little later."

Norm nodded and backed away, signaling her to start the engines. He watched until the Beech Baron roared down the runway and lifted off, gears retracting. It made a left cross wind turn and began climbing.

"Neal, make sure you're buckled in good." Kasey glanced sideways at her passenger. "It's going to get bumpy with that storm out there on the horizon."

"How much longer until we're there?"

"Another forty-five minutes." The plane dropped sharply and Kasey corrected her altitude.

Neal's body tensed and he looked out the window at the ground below.

"Are we going into the storm?"

"Getting nervous?"

"A little."

"Not to worry, I'll get you there in one piece. Just pretend it's a rollercoaster when we drop and you'll be fine. You've been on one before haven't you? Rich boys ride roller coasters too, don't they?"

"Of course I have," Neal answered, his voice reflecting his uneasiness. "But there's a major difference here. The cars on a roller coaster are attached to rails firmly rooted in *terra firma* and we are talking a little difference in altitudes!"

Kasey listened to the voice on her headset updating the weather report. Satisfied with the report, she changed the subject. "Are your parents going to be at your grandfather's party?"

A muscle quivered at Neal's jaw. "No, they're in the South of France on holiday. Even if they weren't on holiday they wouldn't come. They rarely visit the ranch since they have a villa in Sicily and make it their home." Neal sounded curt, distracted as he peered out the window again.

Kasey's mouth formed a silent "o". She *would* have to pick a touchy subject. Oh well, not much further and they would be occupied each in their own way with the landing.

Kasey scanned the sky from left to right, up and down. Pleased there was no air traffic, she took a look at the scenery below. Hills and trees moved below the aircraft and an occasional ribbon of water snaked its way through the landscape, reflecting gold when the sun hit it just right. Ahead in the distance stood a range of snow-capped mountains, the Three Sisters range.

"Damn! What a view!"

Neal raised his head and looked out the front windshield. "I've seen better."

"Oh right, I forgot you've traveled all over the world."

Neal picked up on the sarcasm and said defensively, "I like to travel and I just happen to be in a position to do so. I'm sure you get around, too."

"Nope. Been way too busy trying to keep this company going." *No money, or time for such frivolity*.

The source of Neal Harrison's wealth was a mystery to Kasey, except that he was heir apparent to one of the largest ranches in Oregon, to which they were traveling. She really didn't care to know any other details, but did wonder if it was envy or disdain she was feeling right then. She could surely use the money he wasted to keep her business afloat.

The fact he was a wealthy playboy whose handsome face adorned the society pages of the newspaper several times a month probably entered into her feelings, too. He usually had a beautiful woman on his arm while attending some gala, or was returning from a trip to a foreign country. She had dated him a few times lately, but didn't travel in the same social circles, nor did she care to. So she wondered why he even bothered with her. *Slumming, no doubt.*

Kasey pressed a button on the yoke and spoke into the mike attached to her headset. "Briar Meadows, Baron November six, five, six, Sierra ten miles out for landing advisories." Kasey tossed a reassuring smile at Neal. "Briar Meadows—Baron six five six Sierra ten miles out—landing advisories." Kasey turned her head and scanned from the left. Her gaze continued until she was looking out the window beside Neal.

"Anybody home out there?"

Neal shrugged. "Should be. They're supposed to be expecting us."

"Hi, Baron six five six." A male voice came on the headset barely audible over the static on the radio. "A breeze out of the west. Runway of your choice, we have two. No other traffic."

"Thanks, we'll do a base entry." Kasey turned to Neal, "I'm looking forward to meeting your gran—"

The left engine stopped with a screech and the plane yanked sharply to the left. Neal's head crashed against the door window.

"Ouch! What the shit?" he yelled, grabbing his head.

Kasey looked out the left window. The engine on that side was silent and oil streaks were all over the cowl. The propeller blades were stopped and flat against the wind. She tried to feather the engine but it stayed flat. The oil pressure gauge read zero. She stomped on the right rudder and grabbed the blue and black levers, then eased back with all four. The Baron straightened as the nose dipped.

"What's going on? What's happening?"

Ignoring Neal, Kasey pushed the right blue prop lever full forward then eased the black throttle lever forward. The Barron yawed to the left and she pressed the right rudder pedal.

"Kasey, what the hell is wrong?"

The Baron straightened; the nose came up above the horizon. "I'm busy Neal. Shut the hell up."

Briar Meadows sat in a wide grassy space, framed by a forest of pine, cedar and various other trees. A quarter mile away from the house the runway was a black gash, like a long cigarette burn on a green velvet carpet. The summer sun reflected off a barnlike structure housing a small jet, an apparent hanger a short distance away, completing the picture of the serene haven below. In sharp contrast, however, were the dark clouds hovering on the eastern horizon as the forecasted storm approached.

"Briar Meadows, Baron six five six lost left engine. We'll be doing a straight in. If you have any emergency stuff down there, we will appreciate it. Six five six short final, Briar Meadows." Then to Neal, "Tighten your seat belt and don't move 'til I tell you to unbuckle. You understand?"

"Baron six five six, you should be all right. Will travel the grassy area in case you have to land there. Make sure there are no obstacles."

"That's a roger. Baron six five six out."

Neal cinched his seat belt and shoulder harness. "Done." His voice was thin with fear.

"We'll be fine, Neal. Have a little faith in your pilot." Kasey stole a glance sideways at her passenger when a heavy sigh escaped his lips.

"Maybe under different circumstances."

Although the statement was made with a tone of humor, his manner indicated otherwise. Kasey had been confronted with skepticism often enough to recognize it, but now she had neither the time nor the inclination to defend her abilities.

Neal craned his neck and saw that the propeller still was not moving. "We're going to crash!"

"Neal, try to remain calm. I can't fight you and the plane."

"Calm. Maybe your life isn't all that important, but mine sure as hell is. I should have known some rinky-dink outfit like yours wouldn't be dependable."

"Wait just a minute, Mr. Rich and Famous! We may be a small operation, but we're better than any you'll find. That goes for our pilots, too. I've been flying planes since I was twelve years old and I learned from the best. I'll get your precious butt down safely. Now shut the hell up and let me do my job."

There was a minimum speed at which the rudder would lose power to keep the plane on a straight path, if it got any slower than that, the airplane would just turn left and spiral into the ground. Kasey fought the speed all through the approach as the plane kept trying to turn left toward the bad engine. She put the flaps and gear down and kicked the rudder to the right.

Now it became even harder to keep the plane straight, but Kasey was prepared. She struggled with all the muscle she had left until finally the Beech Baron flew gently above the grassy area beside the runway.

The left propeller was still and the right engine roared. As the ground rushed up to meet them Kasey held firmly to the yoke. The Baron touched down and slid rapidly along the grass toward an ancient water tower at the far end. Neal saw the tower and grabbed for Kasey's arm.

"No, Neal!"

Neal's hand dropped back into his lap. Muscles played back and forth across his cheek as he clenched his teeth. Finally the right engine slowed and the plane rolled to a stop.

Kasey reached over, hit Neal's seat belt release and gave him a nudge. Realizing how tragic the landing could've been, Neal sat for a moment, too stunned to move. He then climbed unsteadily onto the wing, gathering momentum as he jumped onto the ground.

"Neal, hang on a minute. Damn, watch out for the prop!" Kasey yelled through the open door. Neal dodged the prop, staggered a short distance away, bent over and promptly lost his lunch.

A jeep with two men in it drove up and Neal jumped into the back. It turned, maneuvering in front of the Baron and the driver motioned with his arm for her to follow. Kasey advanced the throttle of the right engine and followed the jeep to the hangar where she shut the engine down.

"That was some damn fine jockeying, Miss! I'd like to shake your hand," an old man chortled, his cane swinging in the air punctuating his words. Lofty white brows arched above twinkling blue eyes and beneath a shock of matching hair.

Kasey squatted on the wing. "Thank you, sir. It could have been a damn site worse if it weren't for my ground crew." She jumped down.

"What? Oh, that was Cort over there." He jerked his thumb in the direction of the jeep behind him. "Hell, I haven't seen that kind of flyin' since—well, that's a story I'll have to share with you later. Right now I'd say you could use a stiff shot of brandy." He slipped his arm around Kasey's shoulders and began to lead her toward a pick up truck parked beside the jeep.

"If it's all right with you, sir, I'd like to check out my aircraft," Kasey protested. She glanced toward the other man in the vehicle. *Cort*, the old man had called him. He sat relaxed, one leg hanging from the jeep, watching the scene from beneath the brim of a much worn, black cowboy hat.

Dark eyes surveyed Kasey from head to toe, all five-feet-two inches, before coming back to rest on her face. They took in her faded jeans and tee shirt. The baseball cap on her head with Cimmaron Air imprinted across the front didn't escape the scrutiny either. A half smile tipped the corners of Cort's mouth. The action caused Kasey's body to tingle.

"Thank you, Cort, for your help." She felt self-conscious and wished she had dressed better, but the trip was to have been a quick turn-around; just drop off Neal, gas up and fly back home again.

Cort nodded in acknowledgement, and swinging his other leg around, he untangled his six-foot frame from the jeep. Dusty, scuffed boots peeked from beneath faded jeans that molded with a comfortable ease to his lean, muscled body. A plaid western shirt in varying shades of blue dipped beneath a silver buckled belt at his slender waist. Its sleeves were rolled up to just below his elbows, as if he was prepared to tackle some project.

Hooking his thumb under the brim of his hat, Cort pushed it further back from his brow. He started to speak when Neal got out of the jeep and slipped his arm possessively around Kasey's waist.

"How about my Lady Ace, Cort? I think she's probably as good a pilot as you are, maybe better." Neal laughed, squeezing Kasey against him. He ignored the icy glare Kasey directed his way.

He certainly is showing a change in confidence now that his ass is safely on terra firma, she mused. *True colors, or just an odd reaction to fear?*

"I've no doubt about that, Neal. Looks like you're playing in a better league for a change." Cort's voice was heavy with sarcasm.

"Now, where are my manners? Grandfather. Cort. I would like you to meet Kasey O'Brien. Kasey, this is my grandfather, Spencer Harrison, and," his tone echoed Cort's sarcasm, "this is Cort Navarro, our ranch foreman." He stressed the title as if to put Cort in his proper place.

"Now, boys, you are going to give Miss O'Brien the wrong impression of us." Spence winked, and putting his arm around Kasey's shoulders again, he guided her out of Neal's hold toward her plane. "We may live in the wilderness, but I can assure you, Miss O'Brien, we are civilized. Now, let's have a look at the Beech Baron." Spence dismissed the two men as though they were disobedient children.

The only damage was to the left engine and there wasn't much she could do about that right now. She needed to call Josh and tell him what had happened. With Cort's help Kasey tied down the Baron in case the storm heading their way turned out to be a bad one. Afterward, she used the phone in the hangar to call Cimmaron Air.

"That's right, the left engine seized up," Kasey repeated into the phone to Josh Randall, her friend and the only other full-time pilot working for the company. "Yes, I'm all right. I tied her down for the night. Do you want me to take the engine apart and get back to you with a more detailed report? — Okay, I'll call the National Transportation Safety board first and report the problem to them and let you know what they say—yes, check the engine we just rebuilt. If you can get it in the Cherokee Six, maybe you can bring it along in case. And Josh, call Norm Lang to help out around there. He can cover for you when you come out to get me. Alice can handle the office." Kasey listened to Josh's response. The frustration etched across her face turned to annoyance. "And what does Morley Forbes want now?"

Forbes ran the airport where Cimmaron Air was located. He was about the same age as her father, give or take a year or two. He was not a tall man, maybe five seven, with grey hair that always looked unwashed, combed greasily back in a fifties style. He chewed on a toothpick or matchstick depending on whether or not he had just eaten, and his breath had a rancid odor.

Kasey's father had leased the building from him for the past fifteen years without incident. After Patrick's disappearance though, Forbes' behavior changed toward her. He now considered himself a romantic interest as well as a landlord and it was during one of his more aggressive advances that Neal first entered her life, intervening on her behalf.

Several months earlier, Neal arrived just as Forbes was trying to convince Kasey to kiss him and she wanted no part of it. Neal leaned against the office doorjamb unnoticed and watched to see what would happen next. When the action started to get rough, Neal spoke out. "I don't think the lady wants your attention, partner."

"This is none of your business," Forbes cautioned and he sarcastically added, "partner".

"No? Well maybe it will be the police's business. It won't take a minute for them to get here." He held up his cell phone.

"You *will* regret this, Miss High and Mighty. Mark my words," Forbes warned as he removed his hands from her waist.

Remembering the look on his face as he stormed out of the office still gave her chills. She wanted to have as little to do with him as possible, especially face to face.

Kasey's thoughts returned to her plane. Now was a very bad time for anything more to happen, as if any time was good. First, her father had flown into the side of a mountain nine months earlier, a trauma from which she was still healing. After his disappearance, the business slowed down radically. Patrick had been respected by many people and was good at finding clients, although recent prospects hadn't been as plentiful as in previous years. Now, with him gone, clients were fewer still.

At present, Cimmaron Air was down to two planes — one if the Baron was severely damaged — and there was no capital to replace it. The insurance company was still waiting for the opportunity to recover and examine the wreckage and investigate the accident. They wouldn't even consider paying for the Piper's replacement before then. Kasey wasn't sure how long that would take and was desperately fighting to keep the business from going under, a promise she silently made to her father when she learned of the accident. The way things were going she wasn't sure she could keep that promise. In the meantime, there had been little time to grieve.

On top of all that, she had to deal with Forbes when she returned. Would she have to fend off another romantic advance, or did he want something more extreme—something to do with the business?

"He didn't say what he wanted? Well, just get caught up as much as you can before you have to leave and I'll call him when I get home." Kasey could hear Alice in the background asking Josh if everything was all right. She smiled and told Josh to assure "mama" Greenwood everything was fine.

Josh told Kasey he would fly out as soon as he could, but it wouldn't be for a couple of days. First he had to fly to Arizona and pick up an important shipment for one of their clients.

Kasey hung up the phone, shaking her head. Poor Josh, he was getting paranoid. She could tell by the tone of his voice and by the questions he asked that he didn't believe this was an accident.

Yes, the plane had had a complete going-over last week, but maybe they missed something. Who would tamper with the airplane and why? No, she was not going to let Josh's suspicions influence her thinking, too. It was simply an accident and they would learn more details with the inspection.

Kasey walked around to the left side of the plane. She removed the cowl from the engine, revealing its naked cylinders and other parts normally kept covered. Oil was spattered all over the engine and floor.

Cort knelt down under the engine, looked up and reached his hand toward a shiny hose. A slot had been cut across the steel braided hose and drops of oil hung on the stainless steel slivers.

"Whoa, look at this!" Kasey squatted down beside Cort and looked up to where he pointed. "That's not wear. It had to be cut."

"It sure looks that way, but why would anyone do that? You don't think the plane was tampered with, too?" Kasey reached for the hose. "Ouch! Damn it, that hurt." She inspected her finger and saw a drop of blood.

"Watch it, that stuff's sharp." He took her hand in his and checked the wound. "Too? You said 'too'. Do you think the plane was tampered with?"

"I'm not sure now. Josh thinks so. And that was before he knew about this. Are you sure the oil line's been cut? Maybe is was damaged recently and we never noticed on the inspection."

Cort's eyes narrowed suspiciously and for a moment he seemed to consider something. Changing the subject, he put his hand on a large part with air fin radiators. "Oil cooler?"

"Yep. A lot of oil flows through that thing." Her brow creased with worry. "Man! This is bad. Why would someone cut that line?" She shook her head in utter disbelief. "The NTSB can examine the hose and tell for sure if it's been cut."

"We'd better put this back together for now and leave it for the authorities. I'll drive you up to the house." They stood side by side. "From the looks of the storm approaching, we could be in for an all night siege." His eyes scanned the horizon at the dark clouds looming closer. "Spence took Neal on up to the house and asked me to bring you along after your phone call."

"Thanks, Cort, but I don't want to impose on the Harrison hospitality. Maybe I could get one of the men to drive me into town to get a motel room."

Cort closed the hanger door and shook his head. "It's twenty miles to any form of civilization, and they have no accommodations there. The nearest town with a motel is fifty miles away. That's a good two-hour drive one-way with the condition of the roads as they are now. Once that storm hits, some places will be impassable."

The tall foreman took her elbow, guiding her toward the jeep. "You can have my room until you make other plans. I'm sure Spence would have it no other way. I must warn you, though, I think he is quite taken with you and will probably keep you up half the night telling stories. It's not often he gets a fresh audience." Cort's eyes softened.

"You are very fond of Mr. Harrison, aren't you?"

"If you mean the senior, yeah." Cort looked away lest he reveal too much to this woman he hardly knew. "Did you have any luggage?"

"No, I had no plans to stay."

"No?" One eyebrow arched sharply. "Didn't you come up with Neal for Spence's big birthday bash?"

"Neal did invite me when he hired me to fly him up here. I told him I would bring him, but I wouldn't stay for the party."

"Neal isn't used to taking no for an answer. I wouldn't put it past him to fix it where you would have no choice."

"What do you mean?" Kasey followed his gaze toward the airplane. "Wait a minute, I don't think for one minute Neal would put his life in jeopardy just to get me to stay for a party. Besides, that's a criminal act."

Cort said nothing.

"Look, I have no enemies and our business is not successful enough to be a threat to any of the competition. There must be another answer." A frown crossed Kasey's face as she thought of the possibility. "If by chance what you think is true about the tampering, and I not sure it is, but if by some chance, maybe I wasn't the target."

"You mean Neal? That's possible." Distant thunder rumbled closer as Cort and Kasey pondered the idea. "Come on, let's get to the house."

Kasey eased into the passenger seat, while Cort bent over to secure the seat belt around her. "It's kinda tricky, being as old as it is."

His hand touched briefly against the crease where thigh became hip. The warmth of his touch lingered long after his hand moved on, sending shock waves throughout her body. His nearness made it difficult to breathe.

Cort struggled with the latch, his dark head only inches from Kasey's chin. His scent, a mixture of cologne, sun-warmed hair and the overall intoxicating musk of his body, teased Kasey's senses. Her heart throbbed in her ears until she was sure he could hear it.

An eternity seemed to pass before he finally straightened. "The belt is tricky," he repeated, as a sharp click broke the electrically charged silence. He ran long, strong fingers through his raven black hair, pushing it back from his face. Her gaze followed the gesture, while she wondered if those hands would be gentle against her skin.

Embarrassed by her thoughts about a complete stranger, Kasey looked away. She felt her face color and wondered if Cort noticed. He gave no indication as he hurried around the jeep and jumped into the driver's seat beside her.

Chapter Two

It was late by the time Kasey and Cort arrived at the house. Neal was on the front porch. He informed them that Spence had gone to trouble-shoot a problem somewhere on the vast ranch. Also, the family had eaten but dinner was set for them in the kitchen. Upon hearing his boss had to cover for him, Cort saddled a horse from the corral and set out in the direction Spence had taken.

Kasey ate dinner alone at a small table in the sizeable kitchen. She was a little relieved. It would give her time to unwind before visiting with the Harrisons. She was good at meetings with clients, but had great difficulty when conversations were on a personal level.

In the quiet of the kitchen, Neal's voice came as a surprise. "All finished? Good. I'll take you to your room and maybe you can turn in early. Tomorrow's a big day and you'll need your rest."

"I told you—"

Neal held up his hand to interrupt her. "We'll discuss it later."

Kasey stepped from the black-tiled shower, wrapped herself luxuriously in an oversized cream-colored towel and scooped up her discarded clothing from the floor. Padding into the large masculine bedroom, she draped her clothing across the arm of an over stuffed brown leather sofa that faced the fireplace. It was then she noticed the oil painting over the mantel.

A beautiful young Spanish lady dressed in tight black trousers and matching bolero jacket smiled lovingly at someone beyond the viewer's vision. Her long blue-black hair fanned out behind her, seemingly caught in a strong breeze and frozen at that moment by the artist's brush. One graceful elbow rested on a corral railing, while the other arm hung by her side. A black hat dangled from that hand. Verdant hills rose almost in shadow behind her, a scenic backdrop for the idyllic moment.

"That's Mr. Cort's *mamà*, may she rest in peace," Consuelo Martinez informed Kasey, solemnly making the sign of the cross over her ample bosom.

Kasey whirled around, startled to find she was not alone. Brows knotted in anger at the sudden intrusion. Her expression did not escape Consuelo's attention.

"I'm sorry if I frightened you. I did knock on the door before I came in." She straightened her body to its full four-foot nine height, affronted by Kasey's reaction.

Not wanting to offend the woman further, Kasey answered apologetically, "I'm afraid I was bewitched by the portrait and didn't hear you. She was a beautiful woman."

"Yes, and not just on the outside either. She had a beautiful soul and a heart to match," Consuelo defended, staunchly tapping her chest to punctuate her words.

"Then you knew her? Was this painted here at the ranch?"

"No, she was never here. That was done on her father's estancia in Mexico." Her large brown eyes clouded with visions from the past.

"You were with her in Mexico?"

"I worked for her family."

"How did you and Cort come to work here?" Kasey's face mirrored her puzzlement.

Before the older woman could answer, a knock on the door silenced any further conversation. Consuelo glanced disapprovingly at the towel draped around Kasey's figure. An eyebrow rose as she took it upon herself to answer the door. Consuelo ran her hands down her front, smoothing the white apron, before turning the knob.

"Oh, hi, Consuelo." Neal's cool voice drifted through the partially open door. "I see you have everything under control as usual. I was just checking to see if Kasey needed anything." When Consuelo made no effort to answer him or to offer him entry, Neal laughed softly. "Yes. Well. Tell Kasey good-night for me and I'll see her in the morning."

Kasey self-consciously reached for her shirt and pants, and letting the towel drop to the floor, quickly slipped them on before the housekeeper turned back around. She hid an amused smile behind a raised hand and was glad she did when the housekeeper turned an accusing stare upon her.

"I brought you something to sleep in. I'll take your clothes and have them laundered for morning. Just put them outside the door and I'll pick them up later." Consuelo indicated the pearl pink nightgown lying across the foot of the massive four-poster bed. "If there is nothing else you need, I will leave you to your retirement." This sounded just short of a command.

"Thank you, Consuelo, I think I have everything I need. Good-night." *Does the woman hate everybody or is it just me? What have I done anyway?* Kasey wondered, as the housekeeper closed the door securely behind her. She almost expected to be locked in.

Kasey slipped the satin gown over her head, enjoying the sensation as it slid down her body. Its style, reminiscent of the Harlow era, clung flatteringly to her curves. She could picture the platinum blonde 1930's actress draped across a chaise lounge wearing a gown exactly like this one.

The soft fabric still had that new smell and feel to it. Kasey thought it must get expensive buying clothing for Neal's female guests staying overnight. Suddenly she felt angered at having included herself in the parade of women she assumed he brought here. Maybe that's what set the housekeeper against her. And what about Cort? Did he bring women here, too?

Kasey opened the closet door and ran her hand along the shirts hanging there. She lifted a sleeve and buried her face in it and again smelled Cort's scent. She recognized the cologne from earlier in the day. The room seemed to close in on her.

Her senses reeling, Kasey quickly opened one of the two windows in the room and leaned against the screen, breathing in cool, rain-washed night air. Pungent odors of wet earth and grass, blended with the heady scent of flowers blooming somewhere nearby, refreshed her.

Although it was well after ten o'clock, darkness had only now settled in. She was ready for sleep. The day, long and demanding, had begun when she arrived at the airport before dawn. Kasey had been hoping to catch up on some paperwork before the flight to Oregon. That and the aerobatics later had taken a toll on her.

Most of the storm had passed and now a multitude of stars twinkled in the black velvet sky above. The sight was awe-inspiring. There were too many lights in the San Fernando Valley to be able to see such a spectacle. Distant lightning flashed briefly, illuminating the Three Sisters Mountains to the east. As Kasey watched, a bolt of lightning cut jagged streaks across the far horizon.

Sighing heavily, she turned from the window and with the help of a small footstool from beside the fireplace, she climbed into the grand four-poster bed. It seemed only minutes passed before she drifted into a sound sleep.

Later in the night, Kasey twisted restlessly in bed. Beads of perspiration stood on her forehead and a thin film glistened above her mouth. A soft moan escaped her lips as she became more agitated. Pictures flashed through her mind and she saw her father at the controls of his plane, an eerie outline in the dark cockpit against the faint light of the instrument panel. She sensed his panic and disorientation as he tried to see out the window, then looked back to verify his instrument readings.

She twisted more violently, her lips moving silently as she tried to warn him, but no sound came. Ahead, she saw the dark form of the mountain. There was a blinding flash and the sound of an explosion. She opened her mouth and now a scream tore from the depths of her soul. Kasey sat straight up in bed, jolted awake by the nightmare. She looked around the unfamiliar room to get her bearings.

The bedroom door burst open. Neal switched on the light and hurried to her side as his eyes swept the room in search of a possible intruder. Kasey was pale and trembling. Neal took her into his arms, comforting her.

"I—I had a nightmare," she mumbled against his chest.

Meanwhile, Cort fumbled with the lock on the room's second door that opened to the outside, unaware Neal had entered from the hallway. When he gained access, the scene before him stopped him cold. His mind exploded with dark accusations at seeing Neal's arms around Kasey.

Neal's head jerked around. Recognizing the anger in Cort's face, he released Kasey and stood facing him. "It's all right, Cort. Everything is under control here. Kasey just—"

"Are you all right?" Cort interrupted Neal's explanation. "Is he here against your wishes? Do you want me to get rid of him?"

"It's okay, Cort," Kasey assured hm. "I'm sorry I caused such a scene." Before she could offer any further account, Cort nodded, turned abruptly and strode out of the room.

"I'm afraid Cort thought I was forcing myself on you." Neal laughed nervously. He crossed the room and shut the door, locking it. "I didn't realize he was so gallant. Well, you seem to have two knights in shining armor coming to your rescue. That should do wonders for your ego."

"I'm not sure of the 'shining' part, but I am flattered," Kasey remarked wryly.

A sheen of perspiration coated her body, causing the nightgown to cling seductively. Seeing Neal examine what the damp nightgown revealed, she continued, "Now, if you'll allow me to re-coup my dignity, I'll forever be grateful. I'll explain to Cort in the morning. I don't want him to have any misconceptions about all this."

"What do you care what he thinks?" Neal queried, studying her more closely. "Ah, could it be our cowboy has captured your interest? Let me save you some trouble, Kasey, dear. Cort isn't interested in anything unless it has four feet and whinnies or moos," he finished sarcastically, his glance traveling slowly from her head to the point where her gown dipped into a low vee between her breasts. He bent over the bed again and placed a hand on either side of her.

"Neal, quit it." Kasey put her hand up to stop him. "I appreciate your concern but I have no interest in Cort, or anyone else at this time, if that's any of your business. Since this is his room, I feel the need for an explanation."

"We'll see, Lady Ace, we'll see." Neal glanced at the door through which Cort disappeared and back again at Kasey. "Just remember what I said and you'll save yourself a lot of heartache."

Cort stood on the porch of the bunkhouse, leaning against the support pillar, and stared out into the darkness. He wondered why he had been surprised and then angered at finding Neal with Kasey. After all, she had come here with him like all the others. His first inclination had been to snatch Neal off the bed and knock him across the room, but a niggling voice inside his head stopped him. He was glad now he hadn't made a fool of himself.

Cort pushed away from the pole and walked to the end of the porch. He looked toward the room Kasey occupied, his room. He watched the window, waiting for light to go out.

Though her scream had been one of terror, Kasey had been allowing Neal to hold her. Rather strange behavior if Neal had tried to force himself on her. On the other hand, how had he arrived so quickly? It was certainly not in response to Kasey's scream. Neal's room was at the opposite end of the house and he couldn't have heard her, let alone gotten there so fast.

Cort had been just outside on his way to the bunkhouse and yet Neal was there first. What did it matter anyway? Kasey was just another in a steady stream of women Neal brought to the ranch. She seemed unlike the shallow, plastic creatures that usually graced Neal's arm, though, with their empty smiles and inane chatter. Perhaps she used a different approach with him. If it worked, more power to her. What did it matter to him? He asked himself again. But there was no answer forthcoming.

The next morning after her phone call to the NTSB, Kasey went to the stables looking for Cort and encountered the groom.

"Mr. Cort is down by the lake. He goes there many times," the young man told her, and pointed her in the right direction.

When Kasey asked to borrow a horse, she had to convince him she would be all right riding it by herself. Even then he mumbled to himself while he saddled the horse.

"Miss, I'm going to be in a lot of trouble if you get hurt. Are you sure you know how to ride a horse?"

"I wouldn't do that to you. What's your name?"

"It's Jaime, Ma'am." He brought the sorrel mare with four white socks beside a small platform to help her mount the horse.

"Jaime, it's been a while, but I really do know how to ride."

Kasey held the reins and stepped into the stirrup, swinging her right leg across the horse's rear and lifting herself into the saddle in one smooth move. She guided the horse in the direction Cort's jeep had taken earlier. The tire tracks were easy enough to follow, so she set out in no particular hurry.

It had been years since she rode a horse and Kasey enjoyed the steady, slow gait beneath her. No hustle and bustle of the city out here, no angry impatient customers shouting, no constant drone of airplanes taking off and landing. Nothing but wonderful silence and wide-open spaces filled with warm sunshine and Wedgewood skies.

This would be a good time to explain the events of last night, while Cort was away from the ranch. She didn't know if she should be embarrassed or flattered that there had been two men in her bedroom in the middle of the night, but she wasn't ready for that to be known, especially by the housekeeper. *Why does that woman intimidate me so*?

Kasey ducked under an overhanging branch as she entered the woods and blinked her eyes several times to adjust her vision. Coming from the bright sunlight into the darkness made it difficult to see at first. Through the trees ahead she saw a lake shimmering in the sun and suddenly hoped Cort had some extra fishing gear with him.

It had been a long time since she had been fishing with her father and she had always enjoyed it immensely. Just sitting on the bank with only the sounds of nature around her was the part she liked the best. It didn't matter that she caught no fish.

But when she finally came upon his jeep there was no one in it. She shrugged off her disappointment. Kasey nudged the horse through the dappled sunlight beneath the trees, pulling up on the reins just short of the clearing. Scanning the banks, then the woods, Kasey couldn't locate Cort. She turned the horse down toward the lake and, as she turned, spotted him in the water.

Kasey watched in hypnotic fascination as Cort waded to the bank. He looked like a mythical Greek god emerging from the sea. His body gleamed as beads of water played upon his bare flesh, reflecting the rays of the morning sun. Hardened muscles in his shoulders and chest rippled beneath bronze skin when he stopped and reached skyward in a lazy stretch.

Her gaze slowly traveled the length of his nude body before pausing at the narrow waist, below which the color of his skin abruptly lightened. That part obviously was not as often exposed to the sun. Her inspection continued down the flat stomach and followed a thin line of dark, glistening hair until it widened into a triangle, nestling the ultimate symbol of his manhood.

Kasey flinched. Heat spread rapidly through her body. At the base of her throat a pulse beat an erratic rhythm. A rush of pink stained her cheeks when the heat reached her face.

Suddenly Kasey's horse whinnied and stepped from the cover of the trees. Cort's head jerked upright and dark, snappy eyes looked out from his sun-toughened face. Recognizing the intruder he unwound a lazy, amused smile and walked toward her.

"It seems you have me at a disadvantage, Miss O'Brien. Would you like to join me, or are you just going to sit there in the saddle towering above me and ogle?"

"I'm sorry, I—" Kasey stammered, lowering her eyes. She could feel the color deepening in her cheeks. "I didn't realize—"

"You could at least come down from there and meet me on my level." Cort laughed, closing the distance between them.

"You might cover yourself, too." Kasey was suddenly angry and her embarrassment flared. He was enjoying her discomfort far too much.

"Why? That's like putting on sun tan lotion after you've burned. Besides, I have nothing left to hide."

"I'm sorry, I thought you were fishing. I'll talk to you when— later." Kasey turned her horse around to leave.

"Wait! I'll just put my pants on. It won't take a second. I'm curious as to why you came looking for me. You did come looking for me, I assume?"

"Yes." Kasey kept her back turned to Cort. She could hear the rustling as jeans met bare flesh and the sound conjured up the vision of his nude body once again. It was more than she could bear. She nudged her horse, wanting desperately to get away and he jumped forward.

Cort was immediately beside her, catching the bridle and bringing the horse to a halt. The animal pranced nervously in place, unsettling Kasey, but she managed to regain her seat.

"Been riding long?" Cort asked sharply. "You do know how to ride?"

"I got out here, didn't I?"

"That isn't what I meant."

"I *have* ridden a horse before. It's just been a while."

"How long?"

"Four years ago. Why?" Kasey asked defiantly.

"I mean how long have you been riding?"

"I told you, it was four years ago."

"You only rode a horse once before?" Cort sighed critically, shaking his head.

"I didn't say that." Bitterness crept into her voice. "Why are you so damned concerned with my expertise in horseback riding, anyway?"

"Or lack thereof," he parried. "Miss O'Brien, that horse spooks very easily and there are any number of things in the woods to spook him," Cort continued, a critical tone to his voice. "What if you had been thrown? No one would know where to look for you."

"For your information I told the stable boy where I was going."

"That's beside the point," he interrupted angrily. "From now on you are not to go riding alone. Is that clear?"

"Yes, boss." Kasey snapped her hand to her head, saluting him sarcastically.

Cort straightened, sighing loudly. "Look, Kasey—Miss O'Brien—I didn't mean to sound-highhanded. It's just that you could have been seriously injured and it could have taken a while to find you. Even the best horseman has been known to take a tumble. Just promise me you won't go riding alone again." He hesitated before adding, "Please?"

"Okay. I don't plan on being here very long, and I'm sure I won't have the opportunity again anyway."

"What was it you wanted to see me about?" Cort asked, then seeing the blank look on Kasey's face, he prompted, "You came looking for me, remember. Why don't you come down here?"

Cort moved to Kasey's side, his strong hands circling her waist, and lifted her down. When she was firmly on the ground he released her, putting his hands up, brushing the wet hair from his face. Kasey watched the movement as she had when she first met him. Strange and disquieting thoughts raced through her mind once again.

Lowering her gaze, she watched in fascination as rivulets of water slid in glistening trails down the muscles of his chest. Her cheeks burned in remembrance of what lay in the direction her gaze traveled. Quickly she raised her eyes to find Cort watching her. His steady gaze bore into her in silent expectation. The flush deepened to crimson at being caught again.

The beginnings of a smile tipped the corners of Cort's mouth as he bent over to pick up his shirt. In spite of himself, he was pleased with what he saw in her eyes.

"It's getting late," Cort noted, breaking the uneasiness. "Spence's birthday party is tonight. You'll be there, won't you?"

Aware he was watching her intently, waiting for an answer, Kasey cleared her throat and pretended not to notice his scrutiny. "No. I had planned on leaving right away and I brought nothing to wear. I wouldn't fit in anyway. I'm sure the guest list reads like a society register."

"Nonsense. If I can put in an appearance, so can you." Cort showed no sign of relenting. "I'm sure something can be found for you to wear."

"Yeah, I'm sure," she muttered, remembering the nightgown. "Which reminds me, Cort, about last night."

"You don't owe me an explanation," Cort interrupted, his voice suddenly hardening. A muscle twitched in his jaw and his mouth formed a thin line of displeasure as the vision of Kasey in Neal's arms raced through his mind.

"Will you just hear me out?" Kasey demanded. "I had a nightmare last night about my father. He was killed in an airplane crash a little over nine months ago and, with the engine trouble yesterday— well, I guess it brought the crash back to me." Tears filled her eyes. She swallowed hard, fighting the grief she had managed to control over the months. She didn't want to appear to be one of those hysterical women using tears to her advantage.

"In the dream I was with Pop in the plane. I saw a mountain, and then an explosion." Kasey's voice faltered. "I—I guess I screamed and Neal happened to be nearby. He must have thought I was in trouble or something."

Cort gathered her in his arms. He spoke no words, but his gentleness wrapped around her like a warm blanket. When he finally released her, the tenderness in his expression touched her.

"I'm sorry, Kasey, I didn't know about your father. What happened?" he asked hesitantly. "That is, if you don't mind talking about it."

"I don't know how it happened, but he flew into the side of a mountain. They found the plane a few weeks ago, but the snow was still too deep leading up to it. No survivors, though, they said." She wiped her eyes with the back of her hand, fighting to regain her composure.

"Where did it happen?"

"Vista Montaña, Colorado. They have a small airport and my father went to meet a client there."

Cort stood silently, a question tugging at his mind, but he wouldn't ask her just yet; she had enough to deal with right now. The lines of concentration deepened along his brows and under his eyes, though, as he digested this bit of information.

"Let's get back to the house," Cort suggested. "I want you to come to the party tonight. We can give each other moral support. Besides, Spence will be disappointed if you don't come." He helped Kasey into the jeep and tied her horse behind. Next he moved to help her with the seat belt, but Kasey stopped him, remembering the last time.

"I can manage, thank you." She smiled at him, with only the slightest trace of sadness still visible.

"Tell me about your father. What kind of man was he?" Cort asked, climbing into the jeep and starting the engine.

"He was a big Irishman, with the red hair and temper to go along with it, but he was also a big teddy bear." Kasey smiled lovingly. "I suppose that is one of the reasons our company is working in the red; he was guided more by his heart than his head. I wouldn't have had him any other way, though." She sighed, thinking of the heavy debts facing her and of the disabled plane back at the ranch.

"He was a seat-of-the-pants pilot and one of the best. He was one with the plane and could tell if anything was wrong with it before the problem even showed up. Pop used to tell me the engines talked to him.

"I don't remember anything about my mother; she died when I was five. Pop raised me so I grew up around pilots and mechanics. They were my playmates. My toys were wrenches and mechanics tools. My vocabulary consisted of aeronautical terms and weather forecasts, and my geography lessons were learned on flight maps. But I had more love than children with two parents." Kasey bit her lower lip to quell the tremble and Cort waited quietly.

"He once said to me that he would rather go in a plane crash than die in a rocking chair and at least he got his wish. God, I miss him." Kasey dropped her lashes quickly to hide the hurt, while tears fell unrestricted down her cheeks. *Perhaps,* she thought, *it's too soon to share the memories.* Her sorrow was still a huge, painful knot inside.

Cort lifted his hip and tugged out the handkerchief from his back pocket, passing it to Kasey. "I envy you your childhood. You are fortunate to have had such a father, but then he was just as lucky to have such a daughter. I imagine he felt that way, too."

"Thank you, Cort." She sensed there was something else behind his statement, but he seemed hesitant about adding anything more.

"Well, here we are, pretty lady," Cort announced, pulling the jeep to a stop. "I have to take a trip into town, but I'll expect to see you at the party later." Kasey made a face. "You really have no choice in the matter. Remember, I know where you're staying." Kasey's smile reached her eyes. "That's better. See you later."

*   *   *   *   *   *   *   *

He pounded his fist against the steering wheel, uttering a litany of expletives. After his rage ebbed, he started the engine and backed out of the parking space too fast, almost striking the car parked behind him. Taking a deep breath, he pulled onto the street and merged into traffic. He had hoped Cimmaron Air would be out another plane and the business would go under, the last nail in the coffin so to speak, but he hadn't counted on the bitch being such a good pilot; her old man had been easy.

He laughed at the memory of Patrick's face when he realized what was coming. It had been worth the wait. He had made special plans for Kasey, but if the crash had occurred and she died in it, that would have been okay, too. Now he would have to come up with another idea to bring about the demise of Cimmaron Air to complete his plans.

Chapter Three

Kasey stood before Neal and shrugged hopelessly. "I'm afraid I can't do justice to this dress; it's much too elegant. Maybe I should pass on this party. I'm just not cut out for such affairs."

"Nonsense! You look gorgeous, and I'll be the envy of every man in the room." Neal grinned at her reassuringly. "You have a simple case of the jitters that's all, but they'll pass once you get in there."

Kasey turned to the mirror, studying her reflection. The sea-foam-green dress bared one shoulder and clung sensuously to her body, flaring slightly from her knees to her ankles. Peeking from beneath the hem of the dress were matching high-heeled shoes, anchored by two thin straps. Kasey marveled at the fit. "You must have an inventory that would be the envy of a department store."

"No, I took the liberty of finding out your size from your secretary. I went right out, bought this dress and your nightgown and tucked them into my garment bag with my tux. I wanted to be prepared in case you changed your mind about staying." An expression of satisfaction showed in Neal's eyes.

"You seemed sure I would." A frown pinched her brows together at the thought entering her mind. "Neal, you didn't rig the plane so I would have to stay, did you?"

"I may have a fascination with you, my dear, but it is not a terminal one. We could have died yesterday and I have a definite penchant for living. Besides, what do I know about planes? No more of this nonsense; our guests will be arriving shortly. Are you ready?"

"*Our* guests?" Kasey repeated, her green eyes wide.

"You are my hostess for this bash, and a good choice I might add. By the time Spence tells everyone about your daring feat, you'll be somewhat of a celebrity."

"Oh, Neal, I can't go through with this. I don't know the first thing about being a hostess, and this party is for Mr. Harrison, not me."

"*This party* is in his honor, but I can assure you it is more for family and friends. Spence isn't impressed with these gatherings, or being the center of attention. You'll do fine," Neal assured her, offering his arm. "Ready?"

Kasey was relieved when dinner was announced. Now she could sit down and not worry about remembering names except of those seated near her. Spence pushed Neal aside and offered Kasey his arm. He escorted her through double doors into a long and narrow dining room.

Western art lined the walls here as it did in the great room. Dark wood beams overhead matched the dining table and antique sideboard. A bouquet of exquisite spring flowers occupied the table's center. Crystal stemware sparkled beneath a western-style chandelier, while sterling silver gleamed beside the place settings of Limoges china. Sixteen guests were to be seated for dinner but later more people would join the party for dancing and refreshments.

Her harrowing landing had been told as many times as there were guests around the table. Now, for the most part, Kasey listened to conversations around her and only contributed when asked a question. She felt like a fish out of water. Her world was so different from the world of these people. Unlike them, she had to work for a living!

"Somebody move that damn flower pot in the middle of the table. I can't see the other end!" Spence ordered. Immediately servants appeared, removed the centerpiece, and disappeared once again.

"How're you doing down there, Kasey? Everybody treating you right? Sorry about the seating arrangements but I guess that was all set up before you got here." Spence's voice boomed across the distance and momentarily stopped all conversation.

"I'm fine, Mr. Harrison." Kasey's smile turned to a chuckle when he gave her a conspiratorial wink, letting her know he was aware of her discomfort.

"How about we all adjourn to the other room and get in some dancing to work off this meal?"

Kasey dropped wearily into a chair tucked away behind a large potted palm. She had been unable to draw a steady breath since the people began to arrive, and her head was swimming trying to keep the names with the proper faces. She had been on her feet for what seemed hours since dinner.

Looking across the room at all the "gorgeous people", as she called them, with the fancy gowns and jewels, the elegant hairstyles, she became self-conscious. Her own blonde hair was too short to do much with, and she had brought no cosmetics along.

She took a small mirror from the evening bag Neal had also provided, and gave a quick glance at her face. Her eyes sparkled like emeralds, which she was sure was only from sheer terror. Her cheeks held a rosy glow, again compliments of her emotional state, and the warmth of the room. Of course the glass of champagne had contributed a glow of its own.

Quickly, she replaced the mirror in her bag as three women stopped on the other side of the potted palm.

"Wonder what has become of our lady pilot?" one of the women asked with an amused tone.

"Maybe she fell victim to Monica," another one laughed. "She's certainly in a snit tonight. She's not used to taking a back seat to Neal's attention yet. He doesn't have a long track record with women so she should have known she would get the ax soon enough. S-h-h—there she is. Oh, Monica darling, we were just looking for you." All three women glided across the floor in Monica's direction, while a relieved Kasey eased from her inadvertent hiding place.

"Kasey, child, I have been looking all over for you," Spence called, and he hurried toward her.

"Mr. Harrison, I haven't had the chance to wish you happy birthday yet." Kasey kissed the old man on the cheek. "Many happy returns, and I hope you have many more."

"I don't know if I can handle many more. Besides, at eighty-one I'm pushing my luck a bit."

"Well, you certainly don't look your age, and I truly mean that." And he didn't. He was a tall, slender man with a thinner shock of hair than perhaps he had when he was younger, but it was a beautiful silvery white. His blue eyes had faded some, yet there was definitely a sparkle there that brought a smile to Kasey's lips. His voice held no quiver from age. He walked with a spritely step despite the absence of the cane he had carried earlier.

"Damn," he muttered. "Excuse the language, Kasey, but I was hoping to swap some stories with you. Well, maybe later. Monica is on her way over here, and I have had my fill of her tonight."

Kasey turned toward the approaching woman, wondering how she, too, could avoid her. From the conversation she heard earlier she knew this meeting was inevitable though, but she had hoped—

"Miss O'Brien. There you are. I've been wanting to speak with you all night."

"Call me Kasey, please," Kasey said and smiled thinly. The woman was gorgeous! Classic blonde was the term that came to mind. Cool and elegant, with glacial blue eyes that could look right through a person, and seemed to be turned upon Kasey at the moment.

"I've been hearing about your courageous landing all evening. You are a wonder." Her silky voice was courteous but patronizing at the same time. "Pilot, mechanic, and you own your own business? Is there no end to your talent?"

"I'm afraid it sounds much more elaborate than it really is."

"Now, hostess for the Harrisons." Monica moved closer. "Playing out of your league, aren't you, Kasey?"

"I'm sorry, I don't know what you mean." Kasey realized she had allowed a light bitterness to creep into her voice at the sudden verbal attack.

Monica stood for a moment, her gaze sweeping over Kasey before she continued, "And I wonder what's running through your mind where Neal is concerned? I hope you aren't planning to take advantage of him and his money." Seeing Kasey's stricken expression, she continued, "Oh, I know your business isn't financially stable. And Neal *is* a very generous man." Monica sneered as she delicately fingered her diamond teardrop necklace.

"You know, Monica, I've learned there is no such thing as a free lunch in life. Mr. Harrison paid for my services as a pilot, and he got what he paid for, *at a fair price*." Kasey deliberately looked at the diamond hanging on its twinkling gold chain around Monica's neck and then stared directly into the glacial blue eyes. "I'm not sure *you* can say the same thing, but then, you did say Neal was a very generous man. By the way, what is the going price for sluts these days?" With that Kasey whirled angrily on her heel and went outside.

Kasey took deep breaths of the flower-scented air, trying to calm her frayed nerves. She was angry with herself for being caught up in that woman's game, and also for being rude to Mr. Harrison's guest. *Why did people play such vicious games with other people's feelings?* Again Kasey took deep, calming breaths.

A tall, dark figure stepped from the shadows. "I'm glad to see you caused a little turbulence in there. I've seen heartier folks shot down in flames by that bunch." Cort laughed a full masculine laugh.

"What—oh, hello, Cort. I didn't recognize you with—"

"My clothes on?"

"No! I mean you— the tuxedo, you look different in evening clothes," Kasey stammered, feeling the heat rise to her face, relieved the darkness hid the flush in her cheeks. *Why do I act like a foolish schoolgirl around this man? You'd think I'd never been around a man before.*

"I'm sorry, I didn't mean to embarrass you. It just slipped out. Besides, I thought you could use a laugh just now."

"You heard what went on in there?" Kasey choked.

"Me and a few others."

"Oh, that's just great. I think I'd better go to my room before I make a bigger ass of myself, if that's possible. I'm the world's best at putting my foot in my mouth. Would you please apologize to Mr. Harrison for me?"

"Nonsense, I think you just made his whole year. I left him laughing so hard I thought he would fall out of the chair he was sitting in."

Kasey's hand flew to her mouth. Mr. Harrison must've been in the chair she vacated earlier and heard the whole thing. What if he, too, thought she was after money? "I have to go. Goodnight, Cort."

"No, you don't. I haven't had a dance yet. That is, if you don't mind dancing with the ranch foreman?"

"I can't go back in there."

Hearing the distress in her voice, Cort looked around and offered, "Well, we could dance right here. They are playing a slow dance and if we don't get fancy with the footwork, we should have no problem."

Kasey laughed. "I would like that very much," and she slipped into his arms with ease. *Too much ease*, she thought.

The music wrapped around them, moving them to its rhythm. The outside world no longer existed for Kasey. Being in Cort's arms, feeling the steady beat of his heart against her breast, she felt safe. The problems of the past two days no longer existed, and she wanted to stay in this haven forever.

Cort moved his arms down around her waist, one hand in the small of her back, pulling her closer, and, in a natural response, Kasey slid her arms around his neck. Her soft curves molded to the contours of his lean body. Her head fit perfectly in the hollow between his shoulder and neck. His scent, which lingered in his room, now filled her senses and the feel of him next to her caused her head to reel. She would forever think of Cort when in the future she encountered this fragrance again.

He moved his head until his lips were inches from hers and a trembling began deep inside her, traveling through every nerve in her body. Her breathing slowed and her eyes closed, waiting for the kiss, her mouth hungering for it. Softly as a whisper his lips touched hers.

"I hate to interrupt this touching scene." Neal's mouth twisted into a smirk as he pushed away from the tree against which he had been leaning, watching the couple. "Some of our guest are leaving and I need my hostess."

Hesitantly, Kasey took Neal's arm and allowed him to guide her away. As they entered the house she glanced over her shoulder to see Cort still in the same place, watching them leave. She could not see his face, or his eyes, hard and filled with dislike.

"Somebody got a cigarette?" Cort asked, entering the bunkhouse, his home while Kasey remained at the ranch.

"I thought you quit that," a bunkmate answered.

"I don't want a sermon. I need a cigarette."

One of the men tossed him a package and Cort shook one loose. He threw the pack back and walked out on the porch, looking toward the house.

He flicked a match angrily against the heel of his boot and touched the dancing flame to his cigarette. Drawing deeply, he filled his lungs then exhaled slowly, watching the blue smoke as it floated lazily into the darkness. He waited for the calming effect, but it did not come. Cort was angry with himself for letting this happen again. He determined that Kasey was trying to use him to make Neal jealous, just like the others.

After that first one, Cort had vowed never to let it happen again. He still remembered the pain. Several other women with whom Neal had been involved had tried the same tactic, but Cort discouraged them immediately. Kasey seemed different. What did he care? He would never see her again. She would be leaving soon, and in the meantime it would be easy enough to avoid her.

Cort held the cigarette out, looked at it as if he wasn't sure where it came from, then angrily threw it down and ground it into the dirt with his heel.

Kasey fell onto the couch and rested her head on the arm, stretching her legs full length. So much had happened in the course of the evening, she felt physically drained, but wide-awake. Her body ached in frustration over the feelings Cort stirred in her and left unfulfilled. She had never felt this way about a man. She dated a few when time permitted, kissed and been kissed, but she never loved. *Love. Is that what I feel? Or is it just a physical passion? He is stunningly virile and handsome in a rugged way. How did one distinguish between the two?* She certainly did not know, nor was there anyone she could ask.

How she missed her father! There were so many things they had not discussed.

Kasey pushed herself from the couch and drifted toward the doorway. She was restless and wanted to get some air, get away from the reminders of him permeating the room. How could she think clearly with Cort everywhere?

Outside, she shivered after the warmth of the bedroom. Kasey folded her arms across her chest, rubbing her hands up and down her arms briskly. She looked toward the house. Lights still filled the windows and music drifted down in muted tones. She turned away from the revelry and wandered in the opposite direction, toward the corrals.

Leaning backward against the rails, she looked up into the star-sprinkled sky, as if an answer to her dilemma could be found there. She was so lost in her reverie that when the soft, warm nose nuzzled her shoulder, she gave a frightened cry. The animal reared its head and snorted in alarm.

"Serves you right, you scared me, too," she crooned to the horse, reaching out to rub his nose. "Is the party keeping you up?" The horse snorted. "Me, too."

"You're not going to let that little snob spoil your sleep, are you, Kasey?"

Kasey whirled around at the intrusion. "Oh, Mr. Harrison, I didn't hear you come up."

"Call me Spence, all my other friends do, and I didn't mean to frighten you." The old man put his arm gently around her shoulders. "That little set-to bothering you?" he asked.

"Partly," Kasey answered. "I apologize for making a scene on your special night. It's just that I—"

"Nonsense, I've been waiting for Monica to meet you for a long time and let me tell you it was well worth the wait."

"I don't understand. I've only known you a couple of days," Kasey answered, stopping in mid-stroll to face Spence.

"Oh, I mean figuratively speaking. That Monica was just itching to be put in her place and I have been waiting for the person who could do it. You, my dear, came through with flying colors. I don't believe I could have gotten a better present. You should have seen the look on her face!" Spence threw back his head and roared with laughter.

"I did let a little steam out of her speech, didn't I?" Kasey smiled, fighting back the urge to laugh with him.

"You are a rose among the thorns in my life, little gal, and I am so glad you came. Sorry about your plane, but then someone special like you wouldn't come into my life in any old ordinary manner. No, sirree."

"You are very kind, Mr. Harrison. Spence." Kasey let out a heavy sigh. "Just what I needed right now."

"My grandson been treating you badly? Well, he'll hear from me."

"No, Neal has been—well, Neal. But enough about me, what are you doing out here? Shouldn't you be in there?" Kasey nodded toward the party.

"Hell, no!" Spence exclaimed. "I can't abide all that nonsense. Besides, they're having a high old time and could care less if I'm there. Now tell me what's bothering you."

Kasey let out another deep sigh but she didn't speak.

"You can talk to me. I may not be able to help, but it might feel better to get it out in the open." Spence tilted his head toward Kasey, trying to get a look at her face in the darkness. "Why don't we go back to your room where you can be more comfortable and have a heart-to-heart? I think maybe this will help, too." Spence grinned and slid a bottle of champagne from beneath his dinner jacket.

"Oh no. All I need now is for Mrs. Martinez to find another man in my room," Kasey blurted out. Realizing what she said, she pressed her fingers against her lips.

Spence grabbed Kasey, planted an exuberant kiss on her cheek and roared with laughter. "It's been a long time since I was a threat to a lady's reputation. God bless you for even considering it, but at eighty-one I'm afraid even those memories have long since faded." Spence gasped, brushing a tear from his eyes. "Now, which one did Consuelo chase off, Neal or Cort?"

"Well, actually Neal came to my room while she was there and I wasn't exactly dressed for company. Later both were in my room, and although she wasn't there, I am almost willing to bet she knew about it," Kasey answered softly, lowering her eyes from Spence's amused stare. "But it's not—there was nothing—"

"This I have to hear about. Come on, let's find a place to sit and have some bubbly." Spence led Kasey back to Cort's room. When she was comfortably seated on the couch, he crossed the room and pressed a button on the nightstand to summon Consuelo. He winked mischievously at Kasey and she groaned.

Consuelo transferred two glasses noisily from the tray, to the coffee table, disapproval gleaming in her dark eyes, but she made no remarks this time.

"I think we can manage from here, Consuelo. Thanks." Spence dismissed the elderly housekeeper with a smile and wave of his hand. When she made no attempt to leave, he asked, "Yes?"

"It's close to midnight, *Señor* Spence," she informed her employer and friend.

"I know, Consuelo, but this is my birthday and I'm not finished celebrating just yet." Consuelo raised an eyebrow as her glance took in the champagne and Kasey. "I'll be fine, really." His mouth quirked with humor and he motioned with his hand for her to leave.

"Now, where were we?" He asked after the door closed noisily behind the housekeeper. "Oh, yes, we had just finished talking about Monica, and were discussing the boys visiting your room. I want to hear the whole story."

"Unfortunately, Monica did hit a nerve. I had been thinking about what I could do with just one of the baubles I saw on the women tonight. I mean, with money they paid for it. I'm practical that way."

"There's nothing wrong with that, but let's talk about the boys being in your room. That sounds more interesting right now." He knew it had been a harmless incident as she had said; otherwise he wouldn't have pressured her. Spence certainly didn't believe in prying into people's private liaisons.

Kasey related the nightmare and the following sequence of events while Spence leaned forward to catch every word. Merriment twinkled in his blue eyes at the part where Neal and Cort almost came to blows.

"And did you?" Spence asked when she was finished.

"Did I what?"

"Did you explain to Cort why Neal was in your room?"

Kasey's cheeks flushed and she could feel the heat rising to her face as she recalled her visit to the woods for that purpose. "Yes," she answered simply, her eyes averted from his curious scrutiny. She hadn't even been aware she added that part about the explanation.

"And?"

A knock at the door interrupted the account, much to Kasey's relief, and she rose from the couch more hastily than was necessary.

Cort opened the door and stuck his head in. "Consuelo sent me to convince Spence it's past his bedtime," he explained with a shrug of his shoulders. "She needs her rest, too, and I'm afraid she won't go to bed until the master of the house does."

"Come on in, Cort. Join us for a nightcap."

"Thanks, but I have an early morning and I need a clear head. You really should say goodnight to your guests and get to bed, too."

"All work and no play, Cort, makes for a dull life." He gazed inquisitively into Cort's eyes. Agreeing with Cort, he continued, "I guess you're right, though. Kasey here needs her rest, also. I hear she had a busy night last night." Spence sighed dramatically and then winked at Kasey when she groaned inwardly.

A frown etched Cort's brow and he looked directly at Kasey. "Goodnight, Miss O'Brien. I trust the rest of the evening will pass uneventfully for you." Cort's attention shifted to his employer. "I'll talk to you tomorrow, Spence." Cort pulled the door shut behind him, leaving a noticeable chill in the room.

Kasey was puzzled by his mood. Certainly she had straightened out the misunderstanding about Neal. He had even been charming earlier at the party. What was his problem? The quick, sharp breath Kasey took did not escape Spence.

"Don't worry about Cort's rudeness, Kasey. If he and Neal want to act like fools, they must know I would find out about it. Now, you get some rest and tomorrow I'll take you on a tour of this place." He moved across the room and when he reached Kasey, he stopped, placed his hands on her shoulders and kissed her soundly on the cheek.

"Thanks for one hell of an evening, Kasey O'Brien." Genuine affection warmed his voice. Spence held her at arm's length, looking into her eyes. He started to add something more and then changed his mind. He released her and gave her a friendly pat on the shoulder. When he walked from the room, his movements were suddenly stiff and awkward.

Kasey watched the old rancher leave and wondered what he had left unsaid. What was behind the brief spark of sadness she thought she detected in his eyes? She was all too aware of things left unspoken, deeds left undone, and the grief these things could cause. Unwittingly, a heavy sigh escaped from deep within her soul. She closed the door behind Spence and turned out the lights.

Chapter Four

Kasey awakened early the next morning despite another restless night. Golden sunshine streamed through the window instilling in her an eagerness to be outside. She looked forward to the tour with Spence, since it would probably be the last chance to see the ranch. Hopefully, Josh would be here this afternoon along with the folks from NTSB and the rest of her day would be filled with the examination and repair of her plane. After that she would be returning home, a thought that sparked an odd twinge in the pit of her stomach. She shook her mind free of the idea and dressed hurriedly.

Outside, under the canopy of a cobalt sky, Kasey inhaled deeply, taking advantage of the smog-free air, while she waited for Spence to bring the jeep around. She glanced in the direction of the bunkhouse wondering if Cort was up yet. But then, his day started much earlier and he was probably somewhere on the vast ranch working.

Would she see him while they were touring? She grew hopeful at the idea, yet wondered if he was still angry with her. Was it for telling Spence about the other night? As soon as the thought entered her head, she mentally berated herself for being so concerned about Cort's feelings toward her. In a day or so she would be out of his life and he out of hers.

"Are you ready?" Spence rounded the corner of the house with two horses in tow. "This is a better way to see the ranch and we have a beautiful day for it."

"How lovely! It's going to be a better trip than I imagined."

"That's not all," Spence added, his blue eyes sparkling merrily. "Consuelo packed a wonderful picnic lunch for us." He pointed to the wicker basket strapped behind his saddle.

"You don't suppose she poisoned mine?" Joy bubbled in Kasey's laughter and shone in her eyes at the idea of a picnic and horseback ride. What a wonderful adventure on her last day here! She gave Spence an exuberant hug and, with his help, hastily mounted her horse.

They traveled over the hills and through the stand of trees where Spence pulled up on the reins to show Kasey a beaver pond. A couple of the animals were in residence. She watched one of the beavers swimming across to the lodge they had made in the middle of the pond, where the other worked busily.

A mound of sticks rose out of the water with a circular patch of greenery at the base. The water rippled around the mound, but at the outer edges the pond was smooth as glass, reflecting tall pine trees across the way. Jagged stumps of saplings and small trees jutted out of the water between the lodge and the bank where the horses stood.

Suddenly, the shrill cry of an osprey echoed through the woodlands. It wasn't long until the large bird appeared and hovered at the edge of the far bank. He swooped low just above the surface of the water, touching it with his talons before flying off.

"I have Cort fly a wildlife vet in several times a year to check on the beavers' health. I have great admiration for these guys because they work so hard. Gotta keep them healthy." He grinned, then shifted in his saddle self- consciously.

For a few more minutes Kasey and Spence watched the animals as they worked tirelessly on their dam before turning the horses and heading out into a vast meadow. In the distance, several men were putting fence posts into the ground and Kasey felt a flutter around her heart. Still too far away to distinguish the faces of the men, she felt certain Cort was among them.

"We'll go see how they're doing with the fence and then we'll find a spot for our lunch. Are you getting hungry?" Spence asked, following her gaze.

"I could eat a horse. Oops, sorry about that!" Kasey moaned theatrically. "You don't think I offended them, do you?"

Spence threw back his head and laughed uproariously. "I'd sit a firm seat if I were you. Your horse is eyeballing you with an evil gleam in his eye." He urged his mount forward and Kasey followed.

Still laughing, they arrived where the men were working, and Kasey spotted Cort. He had removed his shirt and perspiration glistened on his skin. She could see the supple muscles ripple in his arms and shoulders as he plunged the posthole digger into the ground. Dark strands of hair fell across his forehead and dirt streaked his face.

At their approach, he lifted his head and dragged the back of one hand across his forehead, wiping the sweat from his brow. He nodded in their direction and offered only a brief glance at Kasey before turning his attention to Spence.

"How's it going, Cort?" Spence asked, dismounting and inspecting the line.

"It's coming along slowly, but surely. What's up?"

"Just showing Kasey around the place. We're going to have a picnic right now. Any ideas about a nice spot?"

Kasey watched the two men, unaware of their conversation. She recalled the other time she had seen Cort with moisture glistening on his body. She let her mind roam and enjoyed the picture it conjured up, comfortable with the knowledge she was unobserved.

A pulse beat at the base of her throat and she put her hand there to quiet it. She was so carried away by her response to him that she failed to hear the jeep approaching until it braked just behind her, sending a cloud of dust swirling about the group.

"Mr. Harrison, you're needed back at the house," the driver announced.

"Well, damn. I'm sorry, Kasey, but all is not lost. Cort can take you on that picnic and bring you back to the house. It's time for his lunch and he probably knows a perfect spot, anyway. We'll have to finish the tour another time." He tossed a wave in the air and climbed into the jeep. Spence grinned and did a high five with the driver as they bumped across the field. "Perfect timing."

"I think I can find my way back." Kasey watched the vehicle pull away. "I don't want to take you from your work."

Cort's eyebrow quirked upward and irritation touched his voice as he answered, "I told you I didn't want you riding alone." His voice softened when he noticed her discomfort. "It's time to knock off for lunch anyway."

Cort chose the beaver pond for the site of their picnic. It was close and afforded shade and water to wash the grime from his body. A grassy area provided a nice cushion for the blanket. Kasey chose to watch the beavers playing a short distance away, rather than evoke more sensations watching Cort wash in the pond. Why reinforce pictures in her mind that would be hard enough to erase once she was at home again?

After they ate the cold chicken, potato salad, cheese and fruit, Cort lay back with his hands behind his head, looking up at the sky. Kasey sat with her legs crossed, sipping a glass of imported Riesling. She listened to the sounds of nature around her with a new awareness, perhaps heightened with the help of the wine. Bees droned nearby where an abundance of wildflowers colored the landscape. Trees with their full summer foliage offered refuge to a varied species of birds, evidenced by the numerous birdcalls. Across the pond was the place she had seen the osprey earlier, and Kasey hoped he would show up again. Immersed in the sounds, Kasey was startled when Cort spoke.

"I'm falling asleep after all that food," he yawned. "How about a dip in the pond?"

"You seem to be in the water as much as you're on the land." As soon as the words were out of her mouth, she regretted them. *Shit,* she muttered under her breath. Another blush crept onto her cheeks. "I didn't bring a suit." She tried to dismiss her embarrassment, but became more entangled in it.

Cort knew what she was thinking and, in spite of his feelings the night before when he watched her walk away with Neal, it gave him a deep sensuous pleasure.

"I've got an idea," he announced, giving Kasey time to recover. "See the large bush over there? You can change into my shirt and your modesty will remain intact. I'm sure it is large enough to hide your uh— delicate sensibilities. Now, who said chivalry is dead?"

When Kasey emerged from behind the bush, Cort was already in the water. She caught sight of his jeans discarded in a heap on the blanket. Her mind was a crazy mixture of hope and fear. *This is crazy ass ridiculous*, she mentally scolded herself. *What is it about this man that brings such perverted thoughts to mind?*

Kasey swallowed hard, lifted her chin and boldly met Cort's gaze while she walked into the water a discreet distance away. Unfortunately, she did not take into consideration how cold the water was. She inhaled sharply, and in her haste to retreat, she slipped on the soft muddy shore and landed with a splash on her bottom.

"You're supposed to rush right in." Cort laughed richly, swimming toward her. "Now, you will have to go in just to get the mud off."

Before Cort could get any closer, Kasey plunged head first into the deep part of the water. Just as quickly, she resurfaced a few feet away. "My God, this water's ice cold!" she gasped, shaking the hair from her face. "How in the hell do you stand it?"

"Swim around; it's great." Cort swam over to her, circling as he watched in amusement. "C'mon, Lady Ace, trust me."

Kasey took his advice and the vigorous movement through the water helped take the chill off as he had promised. She turned on her back and floated lazily on the liquid surface, allowing her breathing to normalize after the workout. In so doing she noticed dark clouds moving in over the trees and thunder echoed across the sky. A flicker of apprehension swept through her and she righted herself.

"Cort, it looks like a storm is coming in. Take me back to the ranch." Her voice was fragile and shaky.

"We can't get much wetter than this." Cort's smile deepened into laughter but then the note in her voice registered. His brows drew downward in a frown. Kasey had a deep fear of storms; he heard it in her voice. He could see it on her face and in her eyes. She wasn't pretending. Cort cast an appraising glance at the clouds and determined they would not have time to reach the ranch before the rain began.

"There's a line shack not far from here." He spoke in a calming voice. "We can stay there until the storm passes. I've stayed there many times during the calving season and while it's not the Hilton, it is comfortable—and dry." He led Kasey from the pond and back to the blanket. Bending over, he grabbed it and wrapped her mummy-like, then briskly rubbed the length of her, drying the moisture from her skin.

Kasey withdrew from his ministrations and sought out her clothes while Cort pulled his jeans over the damp shorts he used as bathing trunks. In her anxious state she hadn't noticed her previous worry had been needless.

Drops of rain hit the weather-worn door of the line shack, leaving dark splotches against the grey wood. Cort pushed the door open and it groaned on age-old hinges against the movement. The scent of moisture on warm earth, mixed with the musty odor of the one-room building, assaulted her senses. Kasey gasped, shivered in panic. Fear, stark and vivid, glittered in her eyes as she gripped Cort's arm.

Chapter Five

"I can't go in there." Kasey's breathing was rapid and shallow. Moisture beaded above her lip and her head whirled as though she would faint.

"What's wrong, Kasey?" Cort slipped his arm around her waist, steadying her with his body. "There's nothing in here, I promise, but if it'll make you feel better, I'll check it out first."

"No, it's not that," she gasped, her breathing becoming more labored. "It's—it's—I don't know—the smell, something—" Flashes of another dark, confining place swept through her mind. Shadowy scary objects, a child's cry, the sounds of thunder tugged at her memory just as she fainted.

Cort caught Kasey when her body slumped against him. He scooped her into his arms and wondered what to do next. Should he take her into the shack that frightened her so? What other choice did he have? It was raining buckets and they couldn't stay outside; there was no other shelter.

Shrugging, Cort carried Kasey effortlessly through the door and to the small cot on the far side of the room. Depositing her unconscious form on it gently, he stepped quickly to the center of the one-room shack and fumbled on the table for the kerosene lamp. He struck a match against the rough wood and touched it to the wick. The light flickered a few times then settled down to a steady glow, pushing back the darkness.

Kasey moaned as she struggled to regain consciousness and Cort was instantly by her side. He bent over her, briskly rubbing her wrists and arms. Her eyes opened and she gazed at him curiously, trying to remember who he was.

"Well, I hope this isn't going to be a new trend, especially when you are around me." Cort straightened, with a sigh. He certainly didn't want to go through that again. "You hyperventilated and it caused you to pass out. What do you think brought that on?"

"I really don't know. I'm always frightened by storms, probably more than most people, but I have never had a reaction like that before. Maybe it's from being too warm or, no, it seems to have something to do with this cabin." She squeezed her eyes shut and re-opened them, clearing away the remnants of the fog. "Just before I fainted there was something—I'm sorry, I don't remember what it was." Kasey got up from the cot too quickly and she swayed. Cort was there at once and caught her. She pointed to the door and he helped her walk across the room.

"It was certainly more than just a fear of the storm to cause a reaction like that," Cort's soothing voice probed. For a moment he studied her intently then started to ask her something else, but changed his mind. No sense pushing her right now. Another day, when the time was better, he would get her to talk about it.

"Looks like the rain is easing a bit and it's a good thing. You're getting soaked."

Kasey took a long, deep breath of the fresh air. "You should have built a porch, then we could have sat on the porch and watched the rain without getting wet. A rocking chair would be nice, too."

"Do you have a porch with a rocking chair, Kasey?" Cort asked, wanting to prolong the peacefulness he saw returning to her eyes.

"No, I wish I did, though. Of course, I wouldn't have time to sit in it. Besides it wouldn't be the same, the peace and quiet, I mean. I live in a tiny apartment above one of the busiest streets in Van Nuys, California."

"You don't sound too happy about that," Cort challenged, suddenly wanting to know more about her. "What would make you happy, Kasey? Marriage—a family? What? What is your plan in life?"

"I really haven't given it much thought." Kasey was surprised by the question and the fact, too, that she hadn't thought much beyond business. "I guess the charter service has taken so much of my time and energy there hasn't been anything left for a personal evaluation."

"Have you thought about selling it before you get in any deeper?" And, seeing the anger cross her face, he added, "Look, I'm sorry, but Neal was shooting his mouth off about your financial problems. He's been looking for an investment and did a little snooping."

"Has he told everybody my business?" She asked angrily. A sudden realization lit Kasey's eyes and her anger deepened. *So, our first date and the questions over dinner were not from concern over my rough encounter with the landlord after all. He had undoubtedly come there to pry and thinking, since I was female, I would be putty in his hands. Why hadn't he just come right out with it? Asked if I was interested in taking on a partner?*

"Kasey, I'm sorry to spring that on you, but maybe it's good you are aware of it. You seem to have enough to worry about without more surprises." Cort took Kasey by the shoulders and turned her to face him. "Is it really that important to you? To risk your pretty neck for a business which, at best, is difficult to keep going, let alone one that's so far in the hole?"

Kasey clenched her fists then relaxed them, anger so close to the surface she felt like screaming. "I can make this business work, make it profitable, dammit. My father started

Cimmaron Air with hardly more than a dream and it's come a long way. I *will* make it work."

"And who are you trying to prove that to? Your father? He's dead, Kasey." Cort dropped his hands and took a deep, ragged breath. "Is this something you want for yourself, or are you trying to live his dream? If you are, what good will it do?" Cort's voice rose in volume and a heart-wrenching pain shadowed his face. "Would he really give a damn? Are you waiting for him to say how proud he is of you? Well, take it from someone who knows, if he never said it before, he sure as hell isn't going to say it now, so what does it matter?"

Cort shook his head abruptly as though ridding his mind of unwanted thoughts. He shut his eyes and pinched the bridge of his nose. When his eyes were wide open again, they were clear, the hurt having been pushed deep inside once more. "Think about it, Kasey, you're a damn good pilot and you're wasting your talent on a business that's going under. And, if you want to know the truth, I think someone is helping it along."

Kasey was breathless with rage at Cort for being so cruel, but then the last thing he said jerked her alarmingly back to the subject she had been avoiding.

"You still believe someone tampered with my plane?"

"Don't you?"

"Why? I told you before, I'm no threat to anyone, and you just told me in no uncertain terms how my business is going under. It's not much of a secret, it would seem. So, who would be concerned enough with a failing business to do something that drastic?" The question hung in the air between them for a seemingly long, silent time. A previous thought she voiced earlier came back to her.

"What if it wasn't me they were after? I'm sure Neal has made some powerful enemies. Being rich and famous, he moves in some important circles. And let's not forget his winning personality, not to mention the trail of broken hearts he's left behind. I met one of them at the party, remember?"

Cort raised an eyebrow. "It's possible, but what about your father's accident? They certainly weren't after Neal then. He wasn't in your life at that time, was he?"

"Who knows? Wait. You think Pop's accident was connected to this? We don't know what happened yet. Besides, he didn't have any enemies."

"None that you know of. Could it be someone he went to meet in Colorado?"

"I don't know who my father went to meet that day. You said Neal had been looking into the business with an interest in buying us out. I have no way of knowing when that began, but if someone was after him and wanted to stop his plans, they probably would've known what Neal was up to."

"That's possible, too. I'll have a talk with him, but in the meantime, if I were you, I'd keep a close watch on my back."

Kasey chewed her bottom lip as she pondered the situation. It made no difference who was after whom, she and her business were involved. She would need to find the money somehow to hire a night watchman to prevent any more tampering with her aircraft. Perhaps Victor would be interested in that job as well; he could sure use the extra money. She said a silent prayer of thanks to her father for sending Victor to her.

Victor appeared at Cimmaron Air the evening her father flew to Colorado. He told Kasey that her father had offered him a job when Patrick was crop dusting in Las Lunas, New Mexico several years earlier. At the time Victor was gainfully employed, but since then he had fallen on hard times and had hitched across the country to take Patrick up on his offer.

The man looked older than his fifty-six years, and his shoulders drooped, causing his stature to appear less than his six feet, and he limped noticeably. Kasey couldn't tell if the limp was caused by the well-worn shoes, which obviously provided little support, or from an injury.

Large grey eyes filled with—what? Kasey couldn't define it. They appeared to be too large for the be-whiskered, weatherworn face. Victor seemed embarrassed by the condition of his tattered clothing, not to mention the grime marking deeper patterns in the lines on his face and hands.

Kasey had felt sorry for him but, while an extra pair of hands was sorely needed checking invoices against shipments and answering the phone when Alice wasn't there, she couldn't afford to hire him full time. Everything was in such an unsettled state the evening he arrived—her father's plane was overdue and attempts to reach him by radio were unsuccessful. Also, extra money was slim to none. So Victor worked many days without pay, saying that when things got better she could make it up to him. At least he would have a roof over his head.

Now she would give him more work and have to find the money somehow. However, she had to make it quite clear he was to take no chances that would put him in danger. If the day before yesterday was any indication, the saboteur, if there was one, was certainly playing for keeps.

Cort was standing with his back against the doorframe watching Kasey's face. Several emotions touched there, bringing changing lights to her eyes. Fingers gripped his heart and squeezed gently. He wasn't going to let this woman get to him. He would not put himself in the position of competing again for the affections of another of Neal's "women". He knew that heartbreak intimately. *What was the saying? 'Once burned, twice shy'?*

"Looks like the rain has stopped. I think we'd better get back to the house," Cort noted, wanting to put some distance between himself and Kasey.

"Good idea. I have a phone call to make." Kasey was anxious to get her business secured, especially since she was tied up at the ranch waiting for Josh, who was doing all the flying right now. Also, poor Alice was holding down the fort by herself and that was a lot of work for the elderly secretary.

Kasey suddenly stood on tiptoe and wrapped her arms about Cort's neck, giving him a friendly hug. Cort stiffened at the action and pulled away uneasily.

"What's that for?" He exhaled the question.

"That's thanks for putting up with my foolishness. I mean, the fainting and hysteria."

"I'm sorry I brought you here and caused all that." His voice was strained and distant. He turned and walked across the yard toward the horses.

Kasey leaned against the door, her mind totally confused by his mood swing. She shook her head to clear the confusion and followed Cort's path. He was already astride his horse and moving away. Fearing the chance of getting lost should he get too far ahead, she quickly mounted her horse and followed silently. Many questions arose in Kasey's mind, but they would have to wait.

As they approached the ranch house, Kasey spotted Neal sitting on the porch railing. His jaw was clenched, eyes slightly narrowed, when he pushed away from his support and moved out to meet them.

"Well, did you have a nice ride?" Neal's voice, quiet and accusing, held an undertone of cold contempt as his gaze swept both of them. "You look none the worse for wear, considering the rainstorm we had."

"We found shelter and, yes, I had a lovely ride, thank you." Kasey accepted his help to dismount, while Cort bent from his saddle and picked up the reins to her horse. He touched the brim of his hat in greeting to Neal and urged his horse forward, leading Kasey's behind him. He did not look in her direction, nor did he say anything to her. For a moment she stared after Cort, a frown pinching her brow. She still couldn't understand why his behavior had changed so drastically *again*.

Neal did not miss the expression on her face and his mood darkened. " I must remind you, Miss O'Brien, Cort is the ranch foreman and has more important things to do than riding around the countryside with you." Neal spat out the words contemptuously.

"Look, Neal, this ride was your grandfather's idea. He was called away and left me in Cort's care. I had absolutely nothing to do with taking the *ranch foreman* away from his duties," Kasey countered, staring directly into his steel-grey eyes.

"The NTSB is here and Spence had to go take care of your business. He has enough to do running this ranch."

"I wasn't expecting them until this afternoon and I thought I would be back before they got here. Would you take me down there?"

"Maybe you'd rather have Cort take you."

Kasey squared her shoulders and placed her hands on her hips. "Stop playing this stupid ass game, Neal! You don't own me, nor are you paying for my time while I'm here at the ranch. I will go riding with whom I please, or do anything else I want. I haven't answered to anyone for my actions since I was a little girl and I sure as hell don't plan to begin at this time in my life." Kasey whirled on her heel and stomped angrily down the steps.

"Where are you going?"

"To my plane to meet with the NTSB guys."

"Wait a minute," Neal called after her. "I'll take you out there, just let me bring the jeep around."

Kasey's steps slowed and she nodded in agreement without looking at him. It was the second time Neal had provoked her anger. This time when she lashed out, she came terribly close to continuing her tirade against him and betraying a confidence with which Cort had entrusted her. Now, she could use the few seconds alone to regain her composure and direct her attention toward the matter of her plane. Josh would be here tomorrow. There would be no time to think of Neal's interference or the disturbing incident that caused her to faint earlier. She would deal with it. Later—

Chapter Six

Kasey sat in the jeep the next morning watching the tiny speck in the air grow larger. Cort had driven the truck and joined them at the hangar. He traded places with Neal in the jeep and rode out to the strip to guide the plane in once it landed. Kasey had insisted on riding with him. Now, she wrung her hands with obvious concern, watching the approaching plane. Cort reached over, putting his hand on top of hers.

"It'll be fine. No one would dare try it again this soon after the other incident unless they are just plain stupid."

"You're probably right, but try telling that to the butterflies in my stomach." She smiled when she heard Josh's voice over the loudspeaker. Her eyes followed the small plane as it got larger and when it landed and taxied back toward them, she could hardly contain her excitement.

Most women had close *women* friends, but Kasey had spent her life around men, so Josh filled that spot for her. In fact, he was more like a brother than a friend. Over the years she had trusted him with most of her innermost thoughts and feelings.

Once Josh was out of the plane, Kasey flung herself into his arms, tears filling her eyes. She was so happy to see him!

"Whoa, Kase, let me get my land legs back or we'll both be picking ourselves off the ground." Josh laughed, then his amber eyes softened as he squeezed her tightly. "It's good to see you, too," he added, his voice reflecting the genuine concern he felt for his friend.

"You don't know how relieved I am to see you, Josh. The flight went all right, didn't it? There haven't been any accidents back home, have there?"

"The flight went great and everything is fine around the office," Josh assured her. "I brought Norm with me to help with the repairs." Josh put his arm around Kasey's waist, drawing her affectionately to his side. "We didn't really have anything pressing and I figured we could use the help."

"Hi, Norm. Sorry he dragged you way out here, but I'm glad you came." Kasey gave him a hug.

"Not a problem. Happy to help out."

Kasey peered through the rear window of the Cherokee Six, her hands shielding the glare at the side of her face. A Continental engine was strapped to the floor. "Did you have any trouble getting it in there?"

"Piece of cake."

"Do you think we'll be able to have things ready to leave in the morning?" Kasey asked, anxious to put the past few days behind her.

"Has the NTSB been here?"

"Yesterday afternoon. They did their examination and filled out the report. The verdict is what we expected. Someone purposely cut the oil line."

"Kase, don't you think you'd be better off staying here for a few more days? I mean, at least until we look into this more."

"No, Josh. If it's me they are after and they want me badly enough, it won't matter where I am. I can't just give up and let the business go under," Kasey argued. "I need to get back to work and there are things I have to arrange. It's been a swell vacation, but —" Just then Kasey caught Cort's gaze fastened on the two of them.

"Oh, Cort, come over here. I want you to meet Josh, our pilot and mechanic. And this is Norm. He helps out in a pinch."

Josh and Cort eyed each other appraisingly as they shook hands. Cort's attention however, was suddenly directed toward the hangar when the phone rang over the loud speaker.

Spence picked up the phone, listened for a moment, then called, "It's for you, Cort."

"Hop in, folks. I need to run over there and get that call, then we'll go on up to the house."

Kasey, Josh, and Norm got out of the jeep and followed Cort into the hangar to check out the crippled plane. She led the men over to where Spence and Neal stood, introducing them. Spence and Josh were deep in conversation and Kasey glanced around to see if Cort had finished his call. She looked just in time to see a frown cross his face. Curious, she tilted her head toward him and heard part of his conversation.

"In Colorado? And how much does he want?" The rest was lost to Kasey when he met her eyes and slowly turned his back to her. After he finished the conversation he replaced the phone on its cradle and walked toward them, his brow still wrinkled with his thoughts.

"Well, let's get on up to the house where Josh and Norm can relax a little before you guys start to work. Consuelo probably has a big lunch ready, too. Unfortunately, I have to go away in the morning and I have some things that need my attention before I can leave. Business, I'm afraid, doesn't follow the polite rules of society. Besides, you have a host who will see to your every need." He patted Spence on the back and walked to the truck.

Spence climbed into the truck with Cort while Neal, Josh, Norm and Kasey got into the jeep.

After lunch Neal drove Kasey back to the hangar since the other men had gone ahead. Through the open doors she could see the engine hanging from a small hoist in front of the Baron, the crew busy around it. Spence hurried to the passenger side and helped Kasey from the jeep.

"Yep, it didn't take the NTSB to figure out someone cut the oil line. Looks like they took a hacksaw to it. Whoever it was knew you didn't have to make a stop and there were no emergency crews or equipment when you got here," Josh said when Kasey walked over to him.

"Someone definitely tried to kill me?"

"Or your passenger. Looks like that's a good possibility."

"And it would have to be someone who is familiar with Cimmaron Air and have access to the planes."

"Yep, or clever enough to get into the hangar without leaving any signs they did."

A shiver ran up Kasey's spine as she took the coveralls Spence handed her. She slipped them on, along with some latex gloves, and walked over to where the work was being done. Josh and Norm lifted the propeller as Kasey guided it to the mount. It was heavy and the men grunted in unison.

"This thing's getting heavier. How're we doing?" Josh asked, his breathing laborious.

"Almost there," Kasey answered. "Just a little bit more."

Thunk. The propeller stopped against metal. Kasey maneuvered a wrench into position and turned the nut, tightening it. "Hang in there. We're doing good."

Darkness settled in as Kasey and crew stood back, eyeing the engine and its propeller. "Wow! That's gotta be a record of some sort," Josh said, wiping his hands on a rag and admiring their work.

"Well, it is for us," Norm answered. "That's the fastest I've ever changed an engine out."

Cort came through the open doors. "How's it going?" He glanced at the left engine. "Work's all done? Good, because Consuelo sent me to tell you dinner can be ready anytime."

"Hi, Cort, we just finished." Kasey brushed her hair back, revealing a grease smudge on her forehead. "Okay, boys, let's get washed up. We can run this thing up in the morning. Right now I'm pretty hungry."

Later that evening, after a fine dinner, Kasey and her crew gathered in the study with Spencer. This room was the senior Harrison's favorite, with its floor-to-ceiling bookshelves, wood panels and massive rock fireplace in which a cozy fire provided the only light in the room. It was a fitting end for an evening of camaraderie before the good-byes. Kasey was sad at the thought, but she tried to put the feeling aside and, for a time, she managed to do so.

"You were going to tell me some of your stories about flying," Kasey reminded Spence, anticipation sparking in her eyes.

Spence exhaled a long sigh of contentment and searched the recesses of his memory. For a time his attention lingered there, before he spoke.

"I'll tell you about the time I learned to fly." Spence picked up his pipe from the table next to his chair. He made a production of filling the bowl with tobacco and lighting it. Perhaps it allowed him more time to draw the story from deep within his mind.

"I was a young man in my early twenties with a wife and baby. I had this job as cook in a supper club in East Texas and I developed a friendship with my boss, Jess Langdon. Several mornings a week Jess and I would get in his plane and fly down into the lower country they called the 'bottoms' to pick up moonshine. He sold it to his special customers at the club. We lived in a dry county, you see, no legal booze.

"We had to fly low and drop down in fields. Lots of times when we got back there would be tassels from the corn tops wound around the wheels. I always paid close attention to what he was doing and I figured if there was ever a time when he started to panic, I was bailing out of there. Those revenuers were a nasty lot and could shoot the plane right out from under you.

"Well, one day we'd just taken off from making our purchase when ol' Jess had a heart attack right there at the controls. He made me grab the yoke before he lost consciousness and I pulled back on those controls so hard we damned near stalled. That was something I was very familiar with. Jess had stalled the engine once making a fast climb out of range of a revenuer's shotgun. I peed my pants that day." He laughed at the memory.

"I knew I didn't want to go through that experience again, so I eased her out level like Jess had explained to me. He was always telling me little things about flying and, like I said before, I watched him closely. Of course, I never thought I would have the need for all that knowledge, or I would've paid closer attention and I wouldn't have been so frightened. I knew I had to land that plane as soon as I found the way back and I don't mind telling you, I wasn't looking forward to that.

"It took me three tries and it was a pretty bumpy landing, but I made it and Jess lived through it. I radioed ahead and they had a doctor waiting for us. After that he taught me everything he knew about flying and I became his pilot. Made a lot of money, too, flying white lightning and other things we won't go into. I invested my money well and that's how I got this ranch. Of course, when I bought this land it was real cheap. We did well, too. Even better after Cort took over." His gaze traveled toward the door and lingered on the shadowy figure leaning against the wall. No one had heard Cort enter the room, but the old man knew he was there and motioned for him to join them.

Kasey's heart skipped a beat and she struggled to gain tighter control of her emotions. His hair was still damp from his shower and he had changed clothes. He wore a light blue denim shirt, open at the throat, displaying wispy curls of the same black hair. Well-worn Levi's hugged his slim hips. Kasey's lips felt dry and there was a roaring in her head that wasn't present before. Unconsciously she drew a deep breath and tried to ignore the strange aching in her heart as the foreman sank into the soft leather couch beside Spence's chair.

Cort casually stretched his long legs out in front of him, crossing them at his ankles. Kasey dragged her attention back to the stories Spence, Josh and Norm shared, each one trying to top the other. Occasionally, though, her gaze drifted back to Cort and each time her heart skipped another beat.

Kasey would be returning home the next morning and she could not afford to let these feelings go any further. The problem was how to stop them. *Will I forget Cort once I return home, back to the daily routine of my previous life? What an odd thought*, she mused, *previous life. When I return will my life be so different? Is that what I'm thinking about?*

"Kase, are you in there? Hello?" Josh laughed. "Are we keeping you up?" All eyes were upon her while the guys waited for an answer to something Norm had asked.

"It's getting late and you folks want to get an early start in the morning," Spence announced, saving Kasey any further discomfort. He stood, offering his hand to help her up from the cushion on the floor and kissed her gently on the cheek. "Pleasant dreams," he whispered in her ear and then gave her a wink.

But Kasey didn't sleep well that night. She suffered through terrible dreams and arose from bed with exhaustion evident in her movements. She turned on the shower, adjusted the temperature, and stood for a long time under the pulsating stream of water trying to revive herself.

Slowly she began to lather the soap against the washcloth and abruptly dropped the bar. Kasey bent to pick it up, but the slippery soap scooted from her grip and in trying to catch it she bumped her head against the wall.

Almost immediately Kasey burst into tears, much to her amazement, and she began to mentally scold herself for being such a baby. *Damned PMS,* she mused. *It must be, but I'm usually ready to take off someone's head not bawl like a baby. Of course the last nine months or so haven't been the best, either.* Kasey thought maybe a good-night's sleep in her own bed and just getting home would do wonders for her emotions, but for now she couldn't stop the tears and she let them flow.

"Kase, are you up? Wake up, lazy-bones."

Kasey barely heard Josh above the sound of the shower. She quickly held her face up to the water, washing away all traces of the tears, then turned off the faucet.

"Just a minute."

"We gotta get going. Time waits for no one, so the story goes." Josh laughed heartily before heading back down the hall, lured by the delicious aroma of breakfast being prepared. He was never one to turn down a meal, although from the looks of his slender frame one would think he missed them frequently.

Dressing quickly in her freshly laundered clothes, Kasey started for the door, then turned one last time to look around the room. When she turned back towards the door, she bumped into Consuelo and gasped in surprise. *Doesn't that woman ever make a noise? At least she could clear her throat or cough or do something.*

"Consuelo, you startled me. I'm glad you're here, though. I want to thank you for taking excellent care of me and for doing my laundry." Kasey looked down at her clothes, then back at the woman. She started to give her a hug, but something in the woman's demeanor prevented her from doing so.

"*Por nada.*" Consuelo entered the room and began to strip the bed linens and prepare it for Cort's return.

Kasey stood a moment staring after Consuelo. "A woman of few words," she muttered under her breath. She made a mental note to purchase something special when she got home and send it to Consuelo as a token of her appreciation, even if the *señora* didn't like her.

Everyone was gathered around the long dining table having breakfast and sharing stories—everyone except Cort. Kasey's heart sank at the thought of leaving without saying good-bye. But then, he left without a word to her. Maybe she was reading more into this than was warranted.

      *   *   *   *   *   *   *   *

Cort taxied the small jet to the edge of the runway and made a right turn. A man held up both arms directing the plane towards him, and after the engine shut down he crawled under the left wing, pulling a rope through a ring there then looped the rope, jerking it tightly.

Getting out of the plane, Cort turned up his shirt collar against the cold wind and jumped down on the tarmac. He hadn't dressed for the altitude. He leaned close to the man, said something, then looked in the direction the man pointed toward the small cafe.

A bell jingled as Cort opened the door and entered the building. A young blond waitress was flirting with a man seated at the counter and when she saw Cort enter, her appreciative eye traveled from his cowboy hat down the length of his body.

Cort tossed his hat on the coat rack and glanced at the red-headed man seated at the far end of the counter. He swung his leg over the stool, settling stiffly on the cushion and reached for the cup turned upside down on a matching saucer. Cort turned it over and nodded as the waitress filled it with hot steaming coffee.

"What else can I do for you, Cowboy?" Her silky voice held a challenge.

"I think that's it for now." A smile ruffled his mouth as he picked up on the innuendo.

The red-headed man scooted his cup and saucer down the counter toward Cort. "You Cort Navarro?" He asked.

"Yeah."

"You got the money?"

"I want to meet this guy first. I want to know if what I'm getting is worth the money."

The red-headed man looked away hastily then shifted on the stool. "That's going to take some time."

"Tell me what you have so far."

*   *   *   *   *   *   *   *

Josh and Norm made a last minute inspection as Kasey looked toward the sky. "I was hoping Cort would be back before we left, but I guess I can leave him a note. I wanted to thank him for giving up his room."

"I wish you would reconsider and let me fly the Baron," Josh said.

"Nope. I don't won't to risk anyone else's neck. I'm quite capable of taking her home. After I write a quick note, we'll be on our way. The sooner we start, the sooner we'll be back and we should get home before dark."

Spence rose from the desk as she entered the hangar. "Sure wish you'd wait. Cort's going to be sorry he missed you. Just got a call from him and he can't get back till tomorrow. Bad weather's got him socked in." He walked toward Kasey and wrapped his arms around her. "I'm sure gonna miss you, girl. I can't say when I've had more fun. Besides, I didn't get to share more of my adventures with you."

"You can always come down to California and see me. I'd love to take you out on the town. Do you think you might be able to get away?"

"Aw, you don't want to be wasting your time with an old codger like me. Maybe I'll just send my grandson instead. Who knows, maybe you'll take a liking to him and become a member of my family," he answered, grinning.

"No offense, sir, but I don't think he is—well, not quite my type."

Spence grinned wider and winked. "Stranger things have happened, and if I know my grandson—"

"Where is Neal, by the way?"

"He went into town last night and I guess he stayed over. Haven't seen hide nor hair of him this morning."

Kasey stood on her tiptoes and kissed the rancher on his cheek and walked away. As she reached her plane she turned back and blew him a kiss.

At the tail of the Baron, Kasey pushed the rudder from side to side before making her way to the open door. Josh helped her up on the wing.

"I can't talk you into letting me fly her home?"

"Nope, I'll see you back at the office. Bet I can beat you there." She grinned mischievously and climbed into the seat. Kasey started the engine as soon as he walked away.

From the air, Kasey took a long look at the ranch as she made a second pass and waggled her wings, then flew down the valley and out of sight.

Spence stood in the same spot long after the plane had disappeared, then slowly turned and went back into the hangar. He picked up the keys to his truck and took one last look toward the horizon before heading back to the house.

"Yep, Lord, I'm gonna miss that girl. Please keep her safe until I can see her again."

Chapter Seven

Kasey had been home three days. While she had agreed not to fly until the mystery of the saboteur was solved, there were still many things to catch up on at the office, so it was late in the evening when she arrived at her apartment. She threw her keys on the hall table and slipped out of her shoes. Bending down for them, she spotted a note lying on the floor. With a long exhausted sigh she picked it up and opened it.

Words were cut from a newspaper or magazine and glued on a white sheet of paper to form the message: UNDERESTIMATED THE PILOT. NEXT TIME, MORE PREPARED.

Kasey's hands trembled as she dialed the phone. "Josh, I just got this note. It says 'underestimated the pilot. Next time, more prepared'. It still doesn't tell me if it's me or Neal he or she is after."

"You think it might be a woman?"

"It could be. Remember that really bitchy woman I told you about who was at the party, the one who was on my case because she thought I was after Neal's money? Well, she could've hired someone to do it; she wouldn't need to know anything about planes in that case. Maybe she was more upset over the break-up than anyone knew. What's the saying about a woman scorned?"

"Kasey."

"I know. I'm grasping at straws."

"Call the police right now and put the note down without getting any more prints on it."

"Okay, I'll call Lieutenant Jerald Blanchard. He's with the Valley police department. He and my father were close friends."

"I'll be there as quickly as I can."

"No, don't come over. I'll be all right. I promise. Josh? Josh?"

Kasey held the phone away from her ear but still heard a sharp click on the other end of the line. She dialed another number and paced the floor as she awaited an answer.

"Hello, I'd like to speak to Lieutenant Blanchard, please. No, it would be better if I speak to him. Will he be long? Okay, will you have him return my call? Yes, it's Kasey O'Brien and the number is 555-4315. Thanks."

Kasey hung up the phone, then jumped when it rang almost immediately. "Hello, Lieutenant. That was quick."

"I'm not a lieutenant, but will I do?"

"Oh, Cort! Where are you?"

"In town. Who is the lieutenant?"

"Lieutenant Blanchard is a friend of my father's on the San Fernando police department. He's the one looking into my father's death and will probably handle the incident with my plane. Are you here in San Fernando?" A click on the line indicated another call was waiting.

"Cort, I'm sorry, could you call back in a few minutes? I think that's the call I've been waiting for. Thanks. It's great hearing from you."

"Hi, Lieutenant. I'm fine. Listen, I got this note — actually it's not really a note but rather a bizarre threat. I assume you saw the report my partner made with your department about the plane incident?"

"Your father's plane?"

"No, not his. Mine. Anyway, I think this might be from the person who cut the oil line."

"Don't touch anything else. I'll be right there."

Blanchard put the note in a baggie with an instrument resembling a pair of tweezers. "Probably no fingerprints on it, but we'll go over it with a fine tooth comb. If there is anything there we'll find it. I'll need a list of people who knew you were going out of town and who would have access to your plane and your apartment."

"There's not many; Morley Forbes, the man who holds the lease to the building, Norm Lang, a pilot who fills in occasionally, Josh, full-time pilot here and my right hand. Then there's Victor Martin who does just about everything around here and Alice Greenwood, part-time secretary. That's about it."

"Well, if you think of anyone else let me know. I'll leave a man outside to watch the building, at least until daylight. Call me if there are any other developments."

"You'll let me know if and when you find out anything?" A knock at the door interrupted the conversation. Kasey looked at Blanchard. He motioned for her to answer it. She pulled the door open.

"Cort! How— Come in." She turned to Blanchard. "Lieutenant Blanchard, this is Cort Navarro. He's the foreman at that ranch in Oregon." She turned back to Cort. "What a nice surprise. I thought you would be calling me back and here you are. How did you know where to find me?"

"Your address is listed in the phone book with your number. What's going on?"

"Well, I think I have all I need here. I'll be in contact with you soon. I'm sure you two have much to talk about. Kasey, keep in touch. Navarro." The lieutenant nodded in Cort's direction. "A pleasure." He stepped into the hallway and pulled the door shut behind him.

"Would you like some coffee, soda?"

"I'm fine. Tell me how things have been going since you returned. Does the lieutenant's visit have anything to do with the oil line incident?"

Another knock sounded at the door. Kasey gave an apologetic shrug to Cort and looked through the peephole. 'It's Josh. I forgot he was on his way over." She opened the door and ushered Josh in.

"I told you that you didn't have to come over."

"I wanted to make sure you were all right. Have the police been here yet?" He glanced across the room. "Hi, Cort. Sorry, I didn't know you were here."

"Yes, worry-wart. He just left and you probably passed him in the hallway. I gave the lieutenant the note and he left a man downstairs to watch over me for the night."

"I see that you are in good hands. Goodnight, Kase. See you in the morning. Hey, Cort, will you be in town long?"

"Just a couple of days. Good seeing you again."

Josh bent down and gave Kasey a kiss on the forehead then closed the door behind him.

"You never answered my question about the lieutenant."

"I was hoping you would forget about that. I really didn't want to raise concern and everything is under control now. However, if you must know," she responded matter-of-factly, "someone left a note under my door, a threat of sorts. Yes, the police are investigating the accident as well and you heard me tell Josh that I have a watchdog out front until daylight. Now that I've answered all your questions, what brings you to our fair city?"

"Business in L.A., and Spence asked me to stop by and check on you. So, I thought I'd call and see if you wanted to go to dinner tomorrow night." He glanced at his watch. "I didn't realize it was so late. I'd better let you get to bed and I have an early meeting tomorrow morning."

Kasey felt a sense of disappointment that Cort didn't come to see her because he wanted to, but at the request of Spence. She didn't reveal those feelings to him, though. "I'd love to have dinner with you and maybe show you my neck of the woods. What time and where?"

"I'll pick you up, I'm old-fashioned that way. Say around seven?"

Cort reached for the door and Kasey put a hand on his shoulder, turning him around. Standing on tiptoe, she touched her lips to his. "It's really good to see you, Cort. Thanks for coming over."

"Be careful. You might not get rid of me so easily," he cautioned and gave her a dimpled smile. He was halfway out the door when he stuck his head back inside. "Will you be all right?"

"Yeah, the watchdog, remember?" She gestured toward the street below. "Oh, how did you get here? Can I drive you back to your hotel?"

"I have a rental. You stay put and lock up. Don't let anyone else in either, especially not me. I might change my mind." He winked and closed the door.

Kasey leaned against the door smiling, arms wrapped tightly across her chest in a warm hug. She was glad Cort had gotten over whatever put him in a bad mood at the ranch.

The phone rang, breaking into her reverie. Kasey wondered who would call her so late, or for that matter who was left to call her? She shook her head in utter disbelief. Her apartment hadn't been this busy in some time.

"Kasey, is Navarro still there?"

"Oh hello, Lieutenant. No, he just left. Why, did you find out something?"

"No, I just wanted to talk to him. Do you know where he is staying?"

"As a matter of fact we didn't get around to that subject, but I'm having dinner with him tomorrow night. Should I have him call you? Is it something I could help you with?"

"Have him call me when you talk to him." Blanchard looked down at the open phone book and, with his finger, traced across the page. The line read O'Brien, Kasey—San Fernando—555-4315.

Chapter Eight

The waiter finished singing a tune from a current Broadway hit and diners applauded. Cort watched Kasey, enjoying what he saw.

"Any news from the police lieutenant?"

"No, except he wants you to call him."

"What about?"

"He didn't say, just that he wanted to talk to you. Now, we're not going to discuss that any further. I don't want to ruin the evening. Tell me about the ranch and Spence."

Cort laughed. "It's only been a few days since you left there." He took her hand in his as he changed the subject. "You look beautiful, Kasey."

"I bet you say that to all the girls." Kasey fluttered her eyelashes theatrically.

"You have a hard time accepting a compliment, don't you? Here, let me show you how it's done. Just say, 'how kind of you' and 'thank you'. See how easy that is. You try it."

"Let's just change the subject, shall we? Tell me what you want to do with your life. We talked about me last time. Remember? The line shack?"

"You mean when you scared the hell outta me? I don't even remember what we talked about — oh, yes I do and we won't go back there. If I remember correctly, you got angry with me." Cort grinned, then looked down at the table thoughtfully. "As for what I want out of life, I haven't thought too much beyond running the ranch. Since my grandfather Navarro is no longer alive, maybe I'll go to Mexico one of these days and see where I began life."

"You've not been back since?" Kasey asked softly.

"Not to the little town where I as born, nor to see the estancia. Of course, there's nothing there for me other than satisfying my curiosity."

"I'm sorry."

"For what?"

"I see pain in your eyes. I heard it in your voice, too, when we were supposedly talking about me that day at the line shack." She placed her hand on his. "Perhaps it's not as bad as you think."

"It is. I'm an outcast there, worse than dead; a bastard," Cort answered bitterly. "But, to use your words, let's not talk about those things anymore. I wish I had time to see your business. Maybe next trip?"

"When are you going back to the ranch?"

"I'm leaving at dawn. Gotta get back."

"Dare I ask when you'll be back this way?"

"I can't say, but it might be when you least expect it." He gave her a smile that sent her pulse racing.

"Well, maybe we can take a quick trip over to Cimmaron Air right now. It's only a mile or so from here. I need to check on a shipment that's supposed to be going out tomorrow anyway."

Cort and Kasey drove up to the large building that housed a hangar, a warehouse and an office. Lights were shinning from the windows and Kasey stepped from the car as soon as it stopped.

"Who the heck's still here?" Kasey frowned.

She tried the door, but it was locked. She dug into her handbag and pulled out a set of keys. Unlocking the door, Kasey pushed it open and glanced around the room.

"Victor? Josh?"

A scraping noise came from the direction of the hangar. Kasey headed through the doorway separating the office from the hangar. She was startled when Cort took her by the arm and pulled her aside, stepping in front of her.

"Is that you, Kasey?" Victor called. "I didn't recognize the car when you drove up. Thought I'd just make myself scarce 'til I found out who it was."

"Oh, Victor, you worried me! I didn't expect anyone to be here this late."

Victor walked closer, his limp very pronounced. He cast a suspicious glance in Cort's direction. "The shipment was late getting here and I wanted to make sure everything was locked up. The invoice is on your desk. I checked the contents thoroughly and it's all in order. The storeroom is locked and everything's secured."

"Victor, this is Cort Navarro, the ranch foreman at Briar Meadows. Cort, this is Victor Martin, my wonderful all around handyman."

Cort extended his hand and Victor reluctantly took it. The pair shook hands while they checked each other out.

"I see you're limping more severely. You haven't hurt yourself moving things around, have you? I told you to just have the shipment put in the office and we'd move it in the morning," Kasey scolded gently.

"No, it's just the weather. All this humidity makes my ankle ache. These old bones don't take kindly to the damp air," he answered, still eyeing Cort. "I was just finishing up here. Is there anything else I can do for you before I go home?"

" No. Go home and get some rest. Don't come in until eleven or so tomorrow. If there is anything I can do for your ankle let me know. And, Victor, thanks." She gave him a hug, her expression one of deep concern for her friend.

"I'll be okay, don't worry your pretty little head. Goodnight." Victor nodded at Cort and left the building.

Cort watched the other man leave before he spoke. "I don't think he trusts me with you."

"Oh, he just has a father complex when it comes to me. Come on, I'll show you around."

Cort looked once again in the direction Victor had taken, then shifted his attention to Kasey and the tour of the building. "What happened to his ankle?"

"He says it's an old injury he aggravated hitch-hiking across country. I keep trying to get him to go to the doctor but he says it'll be all right."

Later that evening Kasey unlocked the door to her apartment and stood aside to let Cort enter. He looked around making sure it was safe, going from room to room turning on lights, checking closets and the shower stall.

"Everything looks okay and the cop is on duty downstairs. I guess you'll be safe enough for me to leave."

Cort took Kasey into his arms, gave her a slow, big hug, then bent his head toward her and kissed her lightly on the lips. Kasey returned the kiss and Cort reluctantly pushed her away.

"I'd better say goodnight while I can."

"Can't you stay for a little while? It's been such a wonderful evening I hate to see it end. Besides, I don't know when I'll be seeing you again."

"I have to leave very early in the morning." He saw the disappointment in her eyes. "Well, maybe just a few minutes, but you promise to kick me out of here in say—" he looked at his watch, "half an hour."

Cort put his arm around Kasey's waist and pulled her against him. His hands slid up her ribs, then he placed them on either side of her face. Looking deep into her eyes for a moment, he kissed her slowly, deeply. Kasey wrapped her arms around his neck, returning the kiss and relaxed against him.

Cort slipped his arms beneath her knees, lifted her up, and carried her into the bedroom. He hesitated, his gaze taking in every detail of her face, before gently setting her on the bed.

"I'm sorry, this was a mistake. I'd better leave before something happens we both may be sorry about later. It's too soon. We both have things that need to be worked out." He seemed pensive, not angry. "I'm not into one night stands or casual affairs, Kasey, and especially if I'm not sure whether it's Neal or me you're really interested in. This was just supposed to be a casual dinner with someone I greatly admire, not a one-shot deal just to satisfy my raging hormones. I don't know if it goes beyond that for either of us. Until I find out—" He shrugged helplessly.

Cort's one serious involvement had ended disastrously and hurt him deeply. He didn't want to make that mistake again. This time he wanted to make sure. With a long exhausted sigh, he blew Kasey a kiss and walked out of the apartment.

Stunned, Kasey sat up on the bed where Cort had left her. A flood of emotions washed over her, from embarrassment to humiliation to anger. She picked up a fringed pillow and threw it at the doorway before burying her face in the spread.

The next morning Kasey eased her car into her parking space at Cimmaron Air. Removing her sunglasses, she glanced into the mirror before turning off the engine. Dark circles tinted the skin below her eyes. She hadn't slept well since her trip to the ranch and last night left her exhausted and disturbed. She shrugged her shoulders and replaced the sunglasses on her nose.

Her head puzzled with the thoughts from last night, Kasey hadn't noticed Forbes' car parked in the parking lot until she stepped from her own car. She cringed. She had forgotten about getting in touch with him. Locking the car door, she stalked into the office, trying to repress her anger. Kasey didn't want to face him first thing this morning, and her mood darkened.

Forbes was sitting in the chair facing her desk. Before acknowledging his presence Kasey marched across the room to the coffee maker, where the brewing liquid filled the air with its delicious aroma. She definitely needed a caffeine boost this morning. Pouring coffee into her red mug, she stirred creamer into it and took her time walking to her desk. She sat down in her chair.

"What do you want, Mr. Forbes? I really am busy right now what with all that's been happening recently."

"I need a word with you and I'm not going to let you off the hook this time."

"So many things have come up lately. I'm sorry. I completely forgot to call you. I promise I'll get back to you in a day or so."

"You know your lease is up soon. I thought we could have dinner and discuss it."

Kasey took a slow sip of coffee before she spoke again. "Would you just draw up the new one and send it to me?"

"Well, now I think we ought to discuss this a little. If not at dinner, maybe in my office where we could have a little privacy."

"Mr. Forbes, I don't have time for this. Send me a copy. I'll give it my utmost attention before I sign and send it back to you." She restrained her anger, but doing so was getting more difficult.

Forbes looked over his shoulder toward the hangar door then leaned across her desk and ran the back of his hand down her cheek. His eyes raked boldly over her body.

Kasey stiffened at his touch and slapped his hand aside. She stood up, walked around the desk and grabbed Morley by the front of his shirt and looked him straight in the eyes. Just then a plane took off and flew low overhead making it impossible to be heard for the moment, but when the noise passed she spat out the words.

"Don't ever touch me like that again or you'll be picking your balls out of your teeth. Get this into your thick head; a relationship with you under any circumstance except strictly business is out of the question." Kasey got in his face. "I'm *not* interested!"

"All right Miss Holier-Than-Thou, you'll be sorry, that I can promise you." He started to leave, but angrily added, "You've snubbed me for the last time, you little whore." He left the building and climbed into his car, burning rubber as he backed out.

Kasey fought to regain control of her emotions. She had neither the time nor energy for this confrontation. If he thought the name-calling and threats would frighten her, he was terribly wrong.

She seethed with mounting rage as she walked over to the filing cabinet and withdrew paperwork. Slamming the file drawer, Kasey threw the documents on her desk and started to sit down.

"Kase, is that you?" Josh called from the hangar.

"Yep, it's me." Kasey left her chair and walked across the office, through the doorway from where Josh's voice came. "Where are you, Josh?"

"Up here. The light's burned out and I want to replace it before I forget."

Kasey turned around and looked up in time to see Josh start down the ladder built against the wall. He was still seven or eight feet up when the rung he was standing on cracked loudly. Before Kasey could scream Josh fell to the cement floor, landing a few feet from where she stood.

Instinct took over as she ran and checked to see if he was breathing. Relieved he was alive, she ran immediately to the phone and dialed 911. Next she called Dr. Hanson and then crouched by Josh, holding his hand. It seemed a long time before she finally heard the wail of sirens. An EMT ambulance and a fire truck pulled up in front and crews from both spilled out of the vehicles, kneeling beside Josh in seconds.

Kasey watched in a daze as the paramedics put Josh's unconscious form into the ambulance and slammed the door.

"He'll be all right, Kasey. I'm pretty sure his arm and maybe his one leg is broken since they took the brunt of the fall, but that nasty bump on his forehead doesn't appear to be as serious as it looks. Of course we'll do x-rays and monitor him throughout the night. He's lucky he fell the way he did. If he'd hit the back of his head instead of his forehead — well, he's a lucky young man," Dr. Hanson assured her, slipping his arm gently about Kasey's shoulders. "Why don't you lock up here and go home?"

"I want to go to the hospital. Josh —"

"Is in good hands. There is nothing you can do for him right now. You'll be much better off if you just go home and get some rest. I promise I'll call you if there's any change."

"I'm so glad your office is close. I feel more assured having you here." She stared after the departing ambulance, its lights flashing and siren screaming. Suddenly, the shrill bell of the telephone summoned her attention.

"Go home, Kasey," the doctor repeated, glancing in the direction of the phone. "Get some rest."

Kasey nodded in agreement when the doctor picked up his bag and made his way to the door. She finished pulling the tall hangar doors together and secured the lock. The phone had finally stopped ringing and she assumed her call messaging had picked it up. Kasey walked back to the door, giving a final shuddering glance over her shoulder at the broken rung of the ladder that had caused Josh's fall. Quickly she flicked off the lights and walked into her office.

"I'm sorry I didn't get here sooner," Blanchard apologized, then held out a hand to Kasey when he saw he had startled her. "Sorry, I thought you saw me pull up."

"I was a little preoccupied, Lieutenant, What can I do for you?"

"I want to have a look at the scene of the accident."

"How did you know?" Tracy led Blanchard back through the office door and into the hangar.

"We go on most calls where an ambulance is summoned. I heard the address and came right over."

"You think they're after Josh, now?"

"Or still after you. It could've been you up there. What was Josh doing way up there anyway?" he asked, looking at the tall ladder.

"Changing the light bulb. It could've been Victor as well. How was anyone to know who would climb that ladder?"

"Indeed. And where is this Victor person?"

"Victor Martin. I told him to take the morning off. He isn't well and I thought he needed the time to rest."

Blanchard started up the ladder, stopping to check each rung as he climbed. Reaching the broken one, he took a handkerchief from his rear pocket and used it to pull at each half of the broken piece of wood. When he could not pry it loose, he took a small pen-light from his shirt pocket and illuminated the broken area.

"How long had that light been out?"

"I don't know. I think it was out last night, but I just don't remember."

Blanchard moved the pen-light from his hand to his mouth. He inspected the nails and break, wrapped his handkerchief around the piece again, wobbled it and pulled half off. He repeated the move with the other half. Then he descended the ladder.

Kasey followed Blanchard into the office where he deposited the two pieces of wood on her desk, placing them together so the crack was still visible. They both examined the broken rung.

"See how the direction of the break is ninety degrees to the way the rung mounts on the uprights." Kasey looked closely and nodded her head. "That tells us the step was removed, laid across some void or propped up against an object. Just enough pressure was applied to fracture the board. Then using the old nails, someone put it back in place so that when anyone over, say, one hundred pounds, stepped on it, WHAM, down they'd come." He slapped the desk to drive home his point.

Kasey blinked hard reacting to the noise and raised her head to look at the lieutenant. "Who?"

"Don't know yet. Up until now I've been looking into the threatening note off the record, but I'm going to talk to the D.A. and see if this is can be added to the investigation. It has to be tied to your plane incident. We've gotta stop this nut before someone gets killed." Blanchard picked up a clasp envelope from Kasey's desk and, using his handkerchief again, dropped the two pieces of wood inside.

"I'll speak with your employee as soon as he is able to answer questions. Maybe he'll remember something that might help us out. I'd like the phone number for this Martin guy, too. Just call my office later; there's no hurry."

"Thanks, Lieutenant, I appreciate your help." Kasey followed Blanchard to his car and watched as he backed away from the parking space, then turned to go back into the office. Troubled by the recent events, she considered closing Cimmaron Air to save anyone else from harm. But if that's what this monster wanted, she would be giving in to him. And *Lady Ace* never gave up a fight.

Kasey glanced up in time to see Neal pulling up in his flashy little silver Mercedes. She groaned inwardly.

"Hey, Kasey, how's it going?"

"Hello, Neal. What brings you out this way?"

"Lunch. Have you had yours yet?"

"You drove all the way out here from L.A. for lunch?"

"Well, not completely. I had a business appointment and I have something I need to talk to you about." He looked after the disappearing car and frowned. "What did the cops want?"

"Josh had an accident and they just took him to the hospital. The police always show up when an ambulance is called." Kasey watched Neal's expression. What exactly she hoped to see was unclear to her. Perhaps she was beginning to suspect everyone with whom she had contact.

"Kasey, I'm sorry about your friend. Is he seriously hurt?"

"I'm not sure. The doctor didn't seem to think so, but I need to go to the hospital and find out for myself. You don't mind if I cut this visit short do you?"

"Well, I had something important —" Neal's car horn signaled he had a phone call. "Excuse me a minute. I won't be long. Please wait. I really need to discuss something with you before you leave."

Kasey watched curiously as Neal leaned in and retrieved the car phone. What was so important that he couldn't simply call her instead of driving all the way out here from his place on Wilshire Boulevard, near downtown L.A.? And why had he not come right out with it instead of asking her to lunch and pretending to be concerned? Kasey had been that route before.

Suddenly, Neal slung the phone into the car, jumped in and sped off, wheels screeching. Not a word to Kasey. No "sorry, I've gotta run", or "I'll get back to you."

"So much for important discussions." Kasey shrugged. In a way she was relieved to be rid of him. Under the best of circumstances Neal was not someone with whom she wanted to share a leisurely lunch, especially after the trip to the ranch where he had showed his true colors.

Massaging her temples, Kasey went back into her office. She walked through the building, checking all the doors again to make sure they were locked and the office secure. She taped a note to the door for Victor knowing he probably was on his way in and couldn't be reached, then rushed to her car.

Kasey hurried from the parking lot into the hospital, stopping to check at the information desk to see which room Josh was in. Surely he would be out of the emergency room by now.

An older woman in a blue smock and white pants manned the front desk. She glanced up and smiled when Kasey approached. "Good afternoon. How may I help you?"

"Which room is Josh Randall in?"

The volunteer entered his name in the computer and scanned the information that appeared on the screen. "Room 312. Go down this hall here to your right. About half way down you'll find the elevator. Take it up to the third floor and turn left when you get off. Check with the nurses' station before you go in because I think they just took him to the room."

"Thanks," Kasey called over her shoulder. She was anxious to see that Josh was all right. Afterwards she would take some aspirin, grab take-out for lunch and go back to the office and try to get some work done. She tapped the button to summon the elevator and tapped it again as though it might make the car come faster. She watched the light indicating its descent and quickly stepped inside once it arrived.

"I'm sorry, Miss, but Mr. Randall needs to rest right now. He's been through a lot down in ER," the unit clerk told Kasey.

"Can't I just peek in and say hello? I won't stay but a minute, I promise. I just need to see for myself that he's okay. Please?"

"I don't think that would be a good idea. Why don't you come back in the morning. It'll be a lot better for him."

Kasey's shoulders sagged. It had been one hell of a day and the thought of leaving without seeing Josh was more than she could handle right now.

The clerk saw the look on her face. "Tell you what, I'll take you down there and you can just pop in and see him for one minute. No more, okay?" Kasey nodded in agreement. The clerk motioned for her to follow and led her a few doors down. She waited at the door while Kasey tiptoed over to Josh's bed.

A large dark bump protruded from his forehead and a wide bandage covered the bridge of his nose. Blue shadows lay beneath his eyes; he was definitely getting shiners. A metal brace lined each side of his right arm, held in place by an elastic bandage. His breathing was a deep, steady rhythm as he slept and he looked so peaceful for someone who had just narrowly missed death.

Kasey leaned over and placed a kiss on his forehead taking care not to touch the bump. Josh stirred, his eyes fluttered open briefly. He mumbled, "Hi, Kase, what're you—" but that was as far as he got.

"Get some rest, Josh. I'll be back later to see how you're doing." He gave her a lop-sided grin and drifted back to sleep.

Kasey left the hospital feeling a little easier about her friend's condition, but she was very perplexed at the turn of events. There were still no answers to her questions of who was doing this and why.

She took her cell phone out and dialed the office number to retrieve her messages. When the greeting started she pressed another number, then her code. Two of the calls were from clients wanting to know about their shipments and requesting return calls, one was a hang-up, but the third one was from Lt. Blanchard. Kasey looked at her watch. His call was placed twenty minutes ago.

"Kasey, I have some very important information for you. Please call me as soon as you can. It concerns your father."

Kasey dialed his number. "What's up?" she asked when Blanchard's voice came on the line.

"Where are you?"

"Just leaving the hospital. What's up?" she repeated.

"I'll meet you at your apartment. I have some news about your father."

"Tell me." Kasey's breath came in gulps and she was not sure she wanted to hear Blanchard's news. On the other hand she desperately needed to know.

"Not over the phone. I'll be there when you get home."

It took Kasey about half the usual time to get home and as she pulled into the garage she saw Blanchard leaning against his parked car. He straightened and walked toward her, offering a hand when she stumbled getting out of the car. Her heart raced and her legs felt weak.

"The search party reached your father's plane and his remains were brought down this afternoon." He paused. When Kasey didn't say anything, he continued, "His body will be taken to the medical examiner's office in Denver and an autopsy will be performed to determine the exact cause of death. They'll be able to determine if he had a heart attack or if the crash killed him, or exactly what happened."

Kasey swayed against Blanchard. The news put to rest the one slim hope she carried at the back of her mind that he would be found alive; that he had survived on sustenance found around him. He had trained for that in Viet Nam.

"Also, the authorities will be putting together the pieces of the plane to find out if there was a malfunction, or pilot error," Blanchard continued and mumbled the last piece of information, but it was not lost on Kasey.

"I can tell you right now, it damn well wasn't pilot error! You should know that. You were his friend." Kasey looked up at the lieutenant, her chin quivering but defiance in her voice.

"Kasey, those aren't my views. The agency has to follow all leads." He touched her elbow lightly. "Let me walk you to your apartment." Blanchard took Kasey by the arm and led her toward the elevator. "Is there someone I can call for you? I'd rather you weren't alone."

"No, not really. Josh is in the hospital and Victor — I'm sure he would be here in a minute, but I would really rather be alone right now." Kasey took a deep breath and rubbed her trembling hands together. "I knew this was coming, but I guess I wasn't as prepared as I thought. I guess you never are."

"Kasey, I've been thinking about your near miss and I was wondering if maybe— Of the people you mentioned, who had access to the company planes? Which ones were around when your father took off?"

"Let me see. Alice and I were here. Victor showed up that evening looking for a job. Josh was in New Mexico on a delivery and Norm was up north on some kind of business. Why, do you think his plane might have been sabotaged, too?"

"Too soon to say. We have to wait until the plane is brought in and thoroughly examined. Also, the medical examiner has to file a report about the cause of death."

"Pop was in perfect health. It had to be the plane—"

The next two days were busy ones for Kasey. Funeral arrangements had to be made and people notified. She decided on a small memorial service since her father's remains would be cremated after the autopsy, according to his wishes.

Josh was out of the hospital and recuperating at his home. Kasey stopped by a couple of times to check on him and keep him updated on everything. Alice spent part of her time there preparing meals for him and making sure he was following the doctor's orders, especially since Josh was having a difficult time adjusting to working with one hand. At least that was one worry off her mind.

The morning of the memorial service the skies were grey and a light California rain was falling. Kasey aroused herself from the numbness that weighed her down and began to dress. She studied her reflection in the mirror as she tried to do something with her hair. It needed a trim, she concluded. She had let it grow longer than she usually did.

Fatigue had settled in pockets under her eyes. Nothing she could do about that right now. She sighed hopelessly and turned away. Going to the hall closet, Kasey pulled out her umbrella and put it by her purse. Her movements were wooden and took much effort. She dreaded the day ahead of her and wished she could just go to sleep until it was over.

A black limousine pulled up in front of Kasey's apartment and the driver buzzed her on the intercom. She picked up her purse and umbrella, checking to see that she had everything before she went downstairs. The driver helped Kasey into the limo where Josh and Victor awaited. The three were silent all the way to the chapel. Alice met them there.

Lt. Blanchard met them out front and took Kasey off to the side. "My men will be around and we'll be keeping a low profile. We want to see if anyone in there acts a little out of the ordinary. I don't know if the person causing the accidents will be there. Sometimes the perps like to see the anguish they cause. We'll be ready if he makes an appearance."

The church was full of mourners. Patrick had many friends and they all seemed to be there. Kasey knew most of them and tried to offer a smile of appreciation as she moved toward the front of the chapel where she would be seated, but a glazed look of despair spread across her face. The full realization of why they were there finally hit her full force. She stumbled. Josh and Victor were on either side of her and each took her by an elbow, steadying her.

The service was a blur and Kasey swallowed hard, fighting back tears as the guests filed by offering their condolences. "Sorry for your loss, Miss O'Brien. Your father was a dear friend and will be missed," was repeated often until one face began to look like the other.

It was all she could do to attend the reception afterward at Alice's home. People milled about, filling their paper plates with a variety of food. A low, steady stream of conversations buzzed around her. Kasey couldn't eat anything. Her throat seemed to close when she even thought about it. She couldn't concentrate, couldn't focus. She just wanted to go home and have this day finished.

Kasey felt the walls closing in and was looking for an avenue of escape when Victor came to her aid, followed by Josh. "Come on, Kasey," Victor said. "We're taking you home. You need quiet and rest."

Kasey followed in a fog of numbness, grateful to her friends for the rescue. Climbing into the limo, she drew a long ragged breath. Her anguish peaked to shatter the last shreds of her control and Lady Ace wept aloud, rocking back and forth. She hoped she would never have to go through anything like this again.

Chapter Nine

Two days after the memorial service, Kasey forced herself back into a routine. She started by going to her father's apartment early that morning to remove his belongings. Since deep in her heart she had harbored the idea Patrick would be home again, she had continued paying the rent. Not wanting to make this final closure on his life when his body was found, she had postponed the job. Now, with his funeral over, she knew it was time. Not that it would be any easier; it was just time.

"Hey, darlin', I told you I would do this for you." Alice scooted across the parking lot and grabbed Kasey in a vise-like bear hug. "You shouldn't have to do this, honey."

"I want—no, I **need** to do this. I will accept your help though." When released, Kasey stood at the door, her stomach pitching as she forced herself to put the key in the lock and turn it.

Kasey had been to his place many times when he was alive, but she never paid any attention to how few personal belongings her father kept. Underwear and socks were stored in a small nightstand with two drawers beside the bed. A photo of him and Kasey, taken two years ago at the airfield, stood atop the same nightstand. She held the photograph close and smiled, remembering that day.

They had just acquired the Cherokee Six in front of which they were standing. Patrick had flown it in moments before, and Kasey and Josh came running out to see it, thrilled that they had a new plane. Josh took the picture, then they took turns flying it around the Valley.

Kasey sighed heavily, tears brimming her eyes, and turned to finish her painful task. Patrick's clothes hung neatly in the closet according to color. The shirts were on one side and the pants on the other. She lifted his jacket hanging from a hook on the door and buried her face in it. His familiar smell still clung to the fabric. Hot tears rolled down her cheeks and dropped onto the jacket, leaving dark blotches.

Alice rushed to Kasey's side, putting her arm around her shoulder, and led her to the sofa. "I'll do that, honey. You go in the kitchen and finish in there."

Patrick didn't own any furniture, having rented the place fully furnished, as he had done the last five times he moved. Kasey had teased her father about having no furniture and moving so often. "I like a change of view every once in a while and I don't want a lot of things I have to take with me," had been his answer.

With the two of them working, it didn't take long to do what was needed in the apartment. Kasey made a note to call the rental company and have the furniture picked up. She would drop the few dishes and cooking utensils by the local cancer society for their thrift shop, along with his clothes. She tucked the photo in a bag and slipped it over her arm. This she would keep.

Kasey hugged Alice tightly. "I couldn't have done this without your help. I'm forever in your debt."

"Nonsense, honey. I was proud to help. You get some rest and eat something. I don't want to lose you, too. I'm really worried about you." She studied Kasey for a moment, then waved goodbye and walked away. Kasey went in the opposite direction to the apartment complex office to give notice to the manager.

Relieved to have that task over, Kasey stopped at the store on her way home to restock her food supply. Afterwards, she went by the cleaners and picked up her clothes. *I should have stopped by and had my haircut. Oh well, too late now.*

When she got off the elevator, Kasey walked down the hall toward her apartment and she heard the phone ringing. She shifted her bundles around and hurriedly turned the key in the lock, pushing the door open. Rushing across the living room, she threw her purse, cleaning and the grocery bag on her sofa and grabbed the phone.

"Hi there, Missy. How about an old codger taking you to dinner?"

"Spence! Where are you?"

"Downstairs. I'm moving into this techie generation, as the boys like to say. Cort loaned me his cell phone. How about dinner?"

"I'd like nothing better. Come on up."

"I have a cab waiting."

"Send him away and come on up. I'm driving."

When Spence stepped into the hall from the elevator, Kasey was waiting for him and she threw her arms around him. "I'm so glad to see you. It's been so —"

"I know Kasey, I know. I'm sorry I couldn't get here sooner." Spence patted her back and held her close. "I've been keeping tabs on you, though."

Kasey wiped the tears with the back of her hand. "How did you get here?"

"I flew down. I had a meeting with my attorney on some business and thought I'd drop by and see you. It's going to be a quick trip, but I had to stop in and see for myself how my girl is doing even though the boys have been checking on you from time to time and reporting to me." He held her at arm's length and studied her face carefully. "I must say I've been pretty worried about you."

"Let me do a quick change and I'll be ready. Make yourself comfortable, I'll be right back."

Spencer wandered around her living room picking up items from a bookshelf and inspecting them. He picked up the urn and noticed the inscription on the side. *Beloved Father and Ace Pilot, Patrick O'Brien.* He quickly replaced it on the shelf.

"I would have been really hurt if you hadn't stopped in to see me. Now I can show you my territory, although it doesn't hold a candle to your place," Kasey called from her bedroom.

"Wish I could do the tour, but I've got to get back. I've been filling in for Cort at the ranch because he's had a lot of business that's taken him away lately. That's one thing that's prevented me from coming to see you sooner. I wanted so badly to be with you through all the troubling times you've had, finding out about your Pop and all," Spence said, just as Kasey rejoined him. "Wow! I forgot how beautiful you are." He took her hand and Kasey spun around before dropping his hand and strutting around the room.

The phone rang. At first Kasey wasn't going to answer it, but she changed her mind.

"Hello." There was only the sound of someone breathing. "Hello. Who's there?" The breathing continued for a few seconds followed by a click as the phone call was abruptly ended. Kasey replaced the phone on its stand and shrugged. "Strange."

Spencer had walked over to the urn again and picked it up while she took the call. When she rejoined him he asked, "Your Pop?"

Kasey's mind was still on the phone call and it took a minute for her to realize Spence had asked her something. "Hm-m-m?" She noted the urn in his hand. "Oh, yes. He wanted it simple. Cremation, a short memorial service and ashes spread over the San Gorgonio Mountains. He's had everything but the last. I'm hanging on a little longer. I'm not completely ready to let go just yet."

Spencer smiled. "That's exactly what I want. Not over San Gorgonio Mountains but anywhere in the Rockies. That part's the family's choice." Spencer took her by the arm. "Now, let's leave all that behind for a while. What do you want to eat?"

"I know this great steak house. It's in an old converted mansion, and if we play our cards just right, we can get one of the back rooms where it'll be quiet so we can visit." Kasey locked the door on the way out and stuck a small piece of colored tape to the top.

Spence filled Kasey in on the beavers' activities and the new animals that had put in an appearance at the ranch. A new colt and several calves were the reason he had been detained. There was always the possibility of complications with new births and either he or Cort made it a habit to be there.

"We thought we were going to have a problem with the mare when she foaled, but just when we were about to give up, he popped right out in my arms. Feisty little devil, too. When I left, he had his head and tail held high and was prancing around the corral like he was king."

"What does he look like? What's his name?"

"He's a roan with a white star in the middle of his forehead." Spencer smiled at the excitement he saw in Kasey's eyes. "We haven't named him yet, but we're open to suggestions."

Their food came and they shared flying stories and laughed. For a short time Kasey's mind wasn't on the tragedies in her life. The evening flew by.

"I think we're gettin' the evil eye for taking up space for so long. They're probably going to charge us rent soon. It's getting late anyway and I have an early morning flight. Why don't you go back with me?"

"I still have the account ledgers to go over and see how much capital we have to work with. I wish now I had been more involved with that end of the business, but Pop said I had enough to worry about and that would be one thing he could take from my shoulders. And I let him, without question." With a note of sadness, she added, "After all, I thought he would be here always." Kasey leaned forward and took Spence's hand. "I wish you could stay longer."

"Another time." He looked at the check and tossed a platinum credit card on it. "That should do it." When the waiter returned with his card Spence signed the receipt, adding a sizeable tip, and took his copy, leaving the original for the waiter. He stood up and went around to pull her chair out. "Now, if you would be so kind as to drop me at my hotel."

"I will, but under protest."

"You know, in my day it was the man who picked up and dropped off when he had a date. I guess if I can move into the techie age I can get over that as well."

Kasey laughed, and then remembering why he had come, she asked. "You said something about seeing your attorney. You have to come all the way to California for a lawyer? Don't get me wrong, I'm glad you did though."

"My nephew is an attorney in Los Angeles and lives in West Lake Village. Your place is a short detour on the way there. He handles all our personal and business legal matters. In case you were wondering, that's why Cort and Neal have dropped by. They were on their way out there and since they had to pass through here, I had them stop by and check on you."

Spencer opened the door for Kasey and hurried around to the passenger side. Silence filled the car on the way to Spence's hotel. When they arrived she clung to him. Comforted in his fatherly embrace, she was reluctant to let him go.

Kasey had only known Spence a short time but she felt close to him, like the grandfather she never knew, but needed right now. She suddenly realized she had traveled through her life without really thinking about relatives. With her father's passing, Kasey had no one and she wondered about her paternal and maternal grandparents. She made a mental note to do some research when she got the time.

Spence studied her face as she backed away from the embrace. A look of tired sadness passed over her features and it tugged painfully at his heart.

"I'm so glad you came," she repeated. "I can't begin to tell you how much it has meant to me. When this is all over I want to come to the ranch again."

"I can't wait. Until then you be careful, and if you need me just call and I'll be here." His face split into a wide grin. "Of course it could get kinda crowded with Neal and Cort here, too." He took her face in his hands and looked deep within her eyes before placing a kiss on her forehead. "Now get goin' so an old man can get some rest." He stood on the sidewalk long after her taillights were eaten up by the traffic, watching with a heavy heart.

Kasey walked down the corridor of her apartment building, her thoughts on her evening with Spence. She took her key out of her purse and started to insert it into the lock when she noticed something was not right.

Ever since the threatening note, Kasey had stuck a piece of colored tape at the top of the door when she left. It was gone. She leaned close to the door and listened, but heard nothing. She placed her hand on the knob and twisted it slowly. The door opened a crack. The intruder could still be in there waiting to kill her. On the other hand, there was no sound from inside her apartment. *Maybe whoever it was took what he wanted and left. Or—this is stupid. I could get killed.*

She went to the end of the hall and called Lieutenant Blanchard. Within minutes he was there with two uniformed officers.

"How do you know someone is in there? Maybe you just forgot to lock the door?"

"If you had doubts why didn't you just ask me that on the phone when I called?"

"Touché."

Kasey explained to him about the tape. "Another thing I just remembered. I got a phone call before I left, but whoever it was didn't say anything. I know someone was there, I could hear breathing."

"Maybe that was to find out if you were home."

"To come over and murder me, or just make sure they wouldn't have interference when they came to rob the place?"

"We'll just have to find that out, won't we?" When Kasey started to follow him into her apartment, he put his hand on her shoulder and pushed her back. "Not until we clear the scene. I don't want to worry about your safety in case someone is lying in wait for your return." He instructed one of the officers to stay with Kasey and then opened the door.

"Kasey, you can come in now but don't touch anything."

Kasey wasn't sure what she would find, so she was quite surprised when everything looked quite normal, except—what? Someone had definitely been in her apartment. She could feel it. It took her a minute to recognize the signs. A throw pillow had been moved and when she went into the bedroom there was a distinct depression in her bed where someone had lain.

"Why would someone come in and sit on my couch and lie on my bed, yet not take anything?"

"Perhaps that wasn't what they had in mind. Maybe whoever it was waited for you to come home. Had you been here like the person thought or come home while he was still here, we'd probably be covering a murder scene right now. At any rate, he left subtle clues that were meant to frighten you. Excuse me, Kasey." Blanchard called for a crime scene unit to come. Maybe they could find fingerprints or other evidence that would give them the identity of the intruder.

"Do you have somewhere to stay for the night? We're going to be working here for a while; besides, I just don't think it's a good idea for you to stay here tonight.

Chapter Ten

Arthur "Red" McNamara listened to the message he had left on the answering device as instructed, then pressed the correct button to indicate he was satisfied with the words and hung up the phone. This was the second message he had left. The previous one was on Kasey's business phone the evening before. Since she hadn't returned that one, he called her again, this time on her cell phone.

McNamara tucked the card on which her phone number was written back in his wallet. He ran his fingers nervously through his hair and looked down at his watch. Maybe Miss O'Brien hadn't checked her messages yet. He had to wait here for her call, so he picked up the phone again, dialed room service and ordered breakfast.

Hopefully, she would get his message and come to meet him. Perhaps what he had to tell her would bring him a sizeable reward. That, combined with what the cowboy was getting together for him, would be his ticket out of the country. The climate here was certainly unhealthy for him in many ways and he was anxious to leave.

A loud knock on the door exploded in the room like a gunshot. McNamara's body jerked uncontrollably. He hesitated a minute, unsure whether he should answer it. If room service was on the other side of the door they sure were fast, but then no one else knew his room number. He had only told Miss

O'Brien and she hadn't answered her phone. He listened for any sound that would tell him who was on the other side of the door, then opened it.

A little over a week had passed since Cort had left her so abruptly and Kasey hadn't heard anything from him. Of course, Spence said he had been away on business trips, but she wanted to talk to him, to hear his voice. She glanced at her watch. Eight o'clock. Josh was opening up this morning, then Alice would be in later. Kasey had planned to take the morning off. She decided to call the ranch before leaving for work to see if he had wrapped up his travels and returned.

An employee answered, telling Kasey Cort wasn't at home right now. Mr. Spencer had gone into town to see friends, the maid informed her, but she was not sure where Mr. Cort was. So Kasey left a message to have him call as soon as he returned. She finished her coffee and rinsed out the cup, then collected her briefcase and locked the apartment. Taking the morning off suddenly lost its appeal.

Victor looked up from a stack of paperwork as Kasey came in. He pushed back the chair and limped quickly around the desk to her side. He had been a tremendous help here at the office, taking a large part of the burden from her shoulders. She wasn't sure she could've made it without him.

"What are you doing here? It's only nine o'clock. You were supposed to be taking the morning off. You should be home resting! I told you I can handle things here for a while. Look at you — you're so pale."

"I know you can, Victor, and you don't know how much I appreciate all that you have done for me." Kasey smiled half-heartedly at him. "I have one more request though." Her cell phone rang.

"Hello. Cort! I'm so glad you called."

"I'm sorry about your father. I came as quickly as I could."

"Where are you?"

"I got your message and I'm on my way to Van Nuys right now." Sounds of traffic could be heard in the background, verifying what he said. "Neal called a week ago and left a message at the ranch that they had reached the plane. I didn't get the message until yesterday."

"How did he know?" She had meant to ask Spence that question also, but somehow the opportunity passed and they never got back to the subject. "That was pretty close to when I found out and I haven't seen or spoken to Neal since before they located the plane."

"He has his ways." Cort left it at that. "Where are you and what can I do?"

"I'm at the office, but I can be home in fifteen minutes. Will you meet me there?"

"Better yet, why don't you wait there? I'll pick you up and we can talk."

"Okay. And thanks, Cort." Kasey returned the phone to her purse. When she looked back at Victor he avoided eye contact and a scowl darkened his face.

"I know you don't trust him, Victor, but he really is one of the good guys."

"Are you sure?" He grabbed a list from the desk and headed towards the hangar area. "Just be careful, that's all I gotta say."

"You're just too protective of me, and I love you for it, but I'm a big girl, dammit." Her cell phone rang again and she grabbed it from her purse. "Are you lost—Oh, hello, Lieutenant. I thought you were someone else. Yes, I can come down to your office. What's this about? Did the results from the autopsy come back?" Kasey bit her bottom lip and her hand trembled as she held the phone to her ear. "I'll be there as soon as I can."

"You want me to go with you?" Victor had stopped and walked back toward Kasey when he heard her side of the conversation. "I can lock up everything around here."

"Thanks, Victor, but I really need you here. We have two shipments coming in this afternoon and they need to be inventoried and made ready to go out tomorrow. Norm is still in New Mexico, I guess Josh is coming in later. He can help you until Norm gets back. Can you tell Cort where I went and have him call me later?"

"You can do that yourself. I think that's him now." He nodded toward the car speeding across the tarmac in their direction. "If there is anything you need just let me know. *Anything*."

Kasey rose up on her toes to give him a hug. "I don't know what I would have done without you, Victor. You've been a lifesaver."

"Just heed my words." He glanced toward the car that had stopped outside the office and then he continued walking toward the hangar.

Cort got out of the car and took Kasey in his arms. Nothing was said; he just held her close for a minute. When he released her, he stepped back and stared at her face.

"You look like hell."

"Gee, thanks, you look pretty good yourself."

"I mean it, Kasey. You need to get some rest."

"I will. Soon. It's almost over now." She took a deep breath, "I need to go to the police station. Will you come with me?"

"What's going on?" Cort asked, a frown creasing his brow.

"I'm not sure, but I'm a bit nervous about it. Lieutenant Blanchard sounded—I don't know, he wouldn't say what it was about over the phone. I've discovered that's usually not a good sign."

Cort put his arm around her waist and led her around the car. Once she was seated he closed the door, hurried to the driver's side, and jumped in.

Blanchard watched through his office window as Kasey and Cort wound their way through the maze of cubicles. He got up and went around his desk, meeting them at the door. He had dreaded talking with Kasey and he had mixed feelings about Cort being with her. He hadn't figured out just how the cowboy fit in with all this yet. On the other hand, he was relieved she had someone with her.

"Have a seat." Blanchard pulled a chair from the corner of the room placing it next to the chair in front of his desk.

"What's this about, Lieutenant?"

"Well, there is no easy way to tell you this. The preliminary autopsy report came back this morning. We put a rush on it since things have been happening." He glanced down at the papers in front of him, then at Cort before returning his attention to Kasey. "A drug turned up."

"You're wrong! My father didn't take drugs. I don't remember him ever taking so much as an aspirin. You've known Pop a long time—did you ever see him take anything?"

"What was the drug?" Cort asked.

"Chloral hydrate."

"Isn't that used in a mickey?"

The Lieutenant's eyes narrowed. "What do you know about chloral hydrate?"

"Not much, other than when it's slipped into a drink it knocks you out. That's common knowledge."

Blanchard glanced at the papers on his desk. "It's also used for nervous disorders or for people suffering insomnia."

"Pop didn't have any of those things. Someone slipped it to him! He definitely wouldn't take anything when he had a flight." Kasey's eyes widened and she took a deep ragged breath. "He was murdered! But why? Who did it? And the accidents lately — are they connected?"

"I'm sorry, Kasey. You wanted to know exactly what they found. I reached the same conclusion about murder, too, especially after the other incidents. "What I can't figure out, beside the motive, is if he was the intended victim, then why the attempt on your life?"

"Don't forget Josh," Kasey added.

"Well, that could have been meant for anyone." Blanchard glanced at Cort, who sat quietly — much too quietly for Blanchard's comfort.

"Any takes on this, Navarro?"

"None. I really don't know enough to comment."

"Hmm-mm," Blanchard answered. He had his suspicions that Cort Navarro was not telling the whole truth. He knew for a fact Cort had been to the same airport in Colorado from which Patrick had flown into the mountainside. He was not ready to ask him about that, though, not until the rest of a background check came in.

"You'll be in town for a while, Navarro?"

"A while, yes. Something I can do for you, Lieutenant?"

"No, not at the moment, but before you leave, get in touch with me."

Blanchard returned his attention to Kasey. "I'm sorry I don't have any more information for you right now. If you can think of anything out of the ordinary that happened the day Patrick left, please let me know right away. Maybe it was something that didn't seem strange at the time." He was interrupted when one of the detectives signaled him. "Excuse me Kasey, Navarro. I'll be right back." Blanchard stepped out of the room and returned a few minutes later. "Sorry, folks, I have to leave. Kasey, I'll get back to you as soon as I learn anything. Like I said, if you think of anything, please get in touch with me."

"How about grabbing a bite to eat?" Cort asked, breaking the silence in the car.

"I'm not really hungry, but thanks anyway." Kasey shrugged her shoulders wearily.

"Did you have breakfast this morning?"

"I can't remember."

"Then you'll have some lunch, even if it's just a bite or two. Maybe some chicken soup. I hear it's supposed to be good for everything." Cort glanced sideways to see if she had any reaction.

"Okay, chicken soup sounds like something I can handle." She smiled and touched his shoulder. "Thanks, Cort, for being here."

Cort pulled into the parking lot of the next coffee shop. Inside he looked at the waitress and pointed to an empty booth. She nodded her head in approval and Kasey slid into the seat. Cort slid in opposite her.

Kasey looked at the menu. "That hamburger looks good — with everything."

"What happened to the soup?" He grinned at her over the menu. "It does sound better than soup though, doesn't it?" He tossed his menu on top of Kasey's and gave their order to the waitress.

After they ate, Kasey reached for her cell phone and got out of the booth. She hadn't checked her messages since the previous afternoon, so she walked over to a more private spot and dialed her office number. When the greeting started she pressed another number, then her code.

"Miss O'Brien, I have some very important information about your father. It is vital that I speak to you right away." The man's tone verified his concern. "My name is Red McNamara and I'm at the Cordova Inn out on the east side of town, room 236. As I said before, it is most urgent I speak to you. Just use the house phone and let me know when you get here. I can meet you in the lobby. And, Miss O'Brien, don't tell anybody else about this. I do mean *nobody*." The message had come in late yesterday after the office closed.

Kasey paled at the mention of her father. Was this a cruel practical joke, or something more sinister? Should she notify the police about this? He had said not to tell anyone, though. What if he was spooked by the police and ran away before she found out what he had to say? The Cordova Inn, being a very public place, would be safe enough, especially if he came to the lobby to meet her.

When Kasey got back to the table she told Cort about the message. "What do you want to do?"

"I want to go find out what this man knows about my father."

Cort pulled a couple of bills from his pocket and tossed them on the table.

Chapter Eleven

Cort and Kasey entered the motel and walked up to the counter. The clerk was busy with another customer, but signaled she would be with them in a moment.

"Thank you for waiting. How can I help you?"

Kasey looked at the clerk's nametag. "Donna, my name is Kasey O'Brien and I'm here to see Mr. McNamara in room 236. He's expecting me. Could you let him know I'm here?"

The clerk stared at them for a moment, then cleared her throat. "I'm sorry, who did you say?"

"Kasey O'Brien."

"No. Sorry, I meant who did you want to see?"

"Mr. McNamara," Kasey repeated.

"Just a moment please." The clerk went to the far end of the counter and picked up a phone. She turned her back to them while she spoke. After she replaced the instrument, she hesitated before returning. "If you'll have a seat over there, it'll be just a minute." Donna indicated chairs in the lobby.

"What do you suppose that was all about?" Kasey asked Cort as they sat down. Before Cort could answer, Blanchard came down a hallway.

"Kasey, what the hell?"

"Lieutenant Blanchard? Did Mr. McNamara call you, too? What does he know about Pop?"

"He called you? How long ago? What did he say?"

"He left a message. I just got it a little while ago. I didn't actually talk to him and I didn't pay attention to the time. I remember that is was after office hours. We close at six. He said he knew something about Pop and it was urgent he speak with me. He wanted me to meet him here at the Cordova."

"From now on, Kasey, please get in touch with me when something like this happens. That's an order!"

"What did he say about Pop? What's going on, Lieutenant?"

"First, I have a picture of a man I want you to look at and tell me if you know him or have seen him before. But I have to warn you though, it's not a pleasant picture."

"How does this tie in?"

"Look at the picture first, then I'll fill you in."

Cort moved behind the chair so he, too, could see the picture. He put a hand on her shoulder to let her know he was there for her.

"Show me the picture." Then as she looked at the photo, "Is he — is he dead?" She shut her eyes. Still, she saw the image of the man lying on the floor, a black hole in the middle of his forehead and all that blood around him.

"Yes, he's dead," Blanchard answered. His gaze moved from Kasey to Cort. For a brief moment, he thought he caught a glimpse of something in Cort's expression as he looked at the photograph. "Do you know who he is?"

"No." Kasey handed the photo back. "Who is he?"

"How about you, Navarro? Know him?" Cort shrugged and shook his head.

"He's Red McNamara, the man who called and left a message on your phone. All his identification is missing, but the clerk at the front desk did identify him as the man who registered under the name of Red McNamara."

Blanchard's eyes remained on Cort as he gave her the information. "We have a rough estimate of the time of death, so I need to know when he called and left the message for you.

We'll be getting the phone records from that room, but it'll take a while for us to get authorization."

"One minute and I'll let you know." Kasey dialed her office and punched in the necessary numbers again to get her messages. She frowned as she listened then said to Blanchard, "It's been erased. I must have done that automatically." Kasey started to put her cell phone away when she noticed there was another message. She had heard a beep earlier indicating a missed call, but before she had a chance to check for a message a call had come through from the lieutenant and she completely forgot the other. Caller ID indicated the number and name were unavailable.

"That's okay, the records we get from the Cordova should tell us. I just thought it would save some time." He glanced at Kasey. "Something?"

"I don't know, Lieutenant. I have a message." Kasey listened as the message came on, her eyes widening. "It's him. It's Mr. McNamara. He called on my cell phone this morning. Early. At six. I must have been in the shower. I don't always check my messages and this morning has been a busy one. He basically left the same message."

"Well, that gives me something to go on until we get more evidence and hear from the coroner's office." He turned to Cort. "Navarro, how long will you be in town?"

"I'm not sure. Why do you ask?"

"I have some questions for you."

"Now is a good time for me."

"Later. I'm waiting for some information to come in and it may prompt other questions. Besides, I'm kinda busy at the moment." He nodded at them. "Kasey, Navarro, thank you for your help. I needed to know if Kasey knew McNamara." Blanchard turned to head back down the hall, but stopped. "Navarro, when did you get into town?"

"Yesterday. Why?"

"Just curious. Is that when you got in touch with Kasey?"

"No, I had business meetings when I got here and I had an early appointment this morning."

Lieutenant Blanchard's eyes narrowed and he studied Cort for a second before continuing down the corridor. He waved a hand over his head when he turned back toward room 236. "Later."

Kasey dropped her head into her hands. "Why is this happening? Who is doing this?"

Cort took Kasey in his arms and propped his chin on her head. "I want you to come back to the ranch for a week or two. I know you'll be safe there. Let Victor and Josh handle the business for a while."

"I won't put them in harm's way just to save my neck," Kasey protested. "This has got to stop before anyone else is killed. I'm going to stay on the Lieutenant until they find out who's responsible. "

"Then close the doors for a couple of weeks."

"And how will I pay my bills? What if my clients don't come back when they have to take their business somewhere else? Their business doesn't stop just because I close my doors for a week."

Cort sighed in surrender. He knew it would do no good to pursue the conversation further. He glanced in the direction Blanchard had taken.

"What do you suppose he wants to ask me?"

"I'm not sure. Do you know anything about any of this?"

"Maybe it has something to do with my knowing about a mickey. Sorry." Cort's expression stilled and grew serious. He seemed distracted for a moment, then he turned her toward the exit.

"Let's get out of here."

A cell phone rang and Kasey picked hers up. She laughed. "Must be yours this time."

Cort patted his pocket and pulled out his phone. He flipped it open and checked the caller ID. "I guess it is." He excused himself and walked a short distance away.

"Yeah, what's up?"

"A package came for you, *M'jito*. It is from a *Señor* McNamara. Do you want me to send it there?"

He listened while Consuelo gave him the information. His brows drew downward in a frown. "No, I'll be there in about three hours." He snapped the phone shut and walked back to Kasey.

"Would you take me back to my office? Today is Josh's first full day at work, even though I told him to wait until next week. I think I might send him home for the rest of the day and I've got work to do."

"Don't you just hate it when no one listens to what you say?" His voice held a note of sarcasm. "Kasey, I have to go back home. Come with me, please? I want to make sure you are safe."

"I thought we just went through that." Kasey stopped walking and looked at him. With an odd twinge of disappointment she added, "I didn't know you had to leave so soon. Can't you stay for a while? You're always in a hurry."

"I thought we just went through that. You know I can't," Cort mimicked. "Sorry, I couldn't pass that up. No, I really can't. Something's come up that requires my immediate attention, but I'll be back as soon as I can. If you change your mind there's still time. I have to get in touch with Blanchard before I leave."

"Not a chance, so it's settled then. I stay. You go."

Cort leaned over and gave her a long kiss. "Lady Ace, you sure can be frustrating at times."

Kasey looked over the numbers in front of her, but her mind wasn't on work. She laid her head down on the desk just as Josh came into the office from the hangar.

"Hey, Kase, what's wrong?"

Kasey raised her head and looked at him. "Ever feel like giving up?"

"All the time, but I'm not going to."

"How's the arm?"

"It hurts like hell at times, but I've had broken bones before. I heal pretty quick." He held his arm up. "At least it's not one of those old bulky casts."

Kasey got up and walked to the soda machine by the door and deposited some coins. Bending over to retrieve the Diet Coke, she glanced outside at the parking lot. She had heard a car drive up and groaned inwardly when she saw Neal get out of his car and walk toward the front door. Josh made himself scarce by ducking into the warehouse.

"Hi, Kasey. Sorry about your father."

"Thanks, Neal." Kasey noted his uneasiness and attributed it to the fact he was unaccustomed to being kind. "Have a seat."

He hesitated, measuring her for a moment, then sat down in the chair. "I have some unpleasant business to go over with you. Sorry it has to be right now, but you'll find out about it soon enough. I'd rather it come from me."

Icy fear twisted around her heart as she prepared for more bad news. "Did something happen to Cort? Was there an accident? Is Spence okay?"

"No. Your cowboy is on his way to the ranch, I suppose, and my grandfather is fine."

What could possibly be left? Kasey sighed heavily and walked back around her desk, taking the chair she had just vacated.

"A while back your father borrowed money from me. He put up the business as collateral." He paused for a moment. "I will be filing against his estate to collect that money."

"How much was it?" Kasey asked, feeling as though her breath had been knocked from her. She searched her memory to figure out when this possibly could have happened since she had never heard of Neal until after her father went missing.

Then she realized her previous suspicions about him were confirmed. Neal's prior attentions had not been as a caring friend or potential lover, and she was furious at his deception. "How come you never mentioned this before? Why didn't you just come right out and tell me at the beginning instead of making me think something else motivated your — " Humiliation at her gullibility prevented Kasey from finishing the question. Of course! A person in his position wouldn't look at her in a romantic way; she should have known that. She was embarrassed for having ever considered it a possibility.

"In answer to your first question, he borrowed one hundred and fifty thousand dollars eighteen months ago, a few months before he went missing." Neal handed her a copy of the promissory note.

"A hundred and fifty thousand?" Panic stricken, Kasey gasped. She glanced at the paper with unseeing eyes. It was too much for her to comprehend right now. A tumble of confused feelings and thoughts assailed her. When had that amount of money come into the business? And where was it? Were they in debt that much?

Kasey had never been involved in the financial part of Cimmaron Air. She just flew the planes, looked after the mechanical upkeep and helped with shipments. Her father kept the books. Surely one of the ledgers in front of her would shed some light on all of this.

"He paid enough to equal three months worth of payments then had another payment postponed, but now it's incredibly in arrears. There's interest, too," Neal continued. "I didn't want to bother you with the details because you had enough to deal with at the time." He took the promissory note from Kasey's hand and put it back in his briefcase.

"How did—what made him go to you for a loan?"

"Have you seen the ads in the classified section of the paper—the little two or three liners that offer loans for small businesses? That's one of my sidelines. Your father came to me for the money." He shifted uneasily in his chair.

"I see, and then when people can't pay the loan back you swoop down on them like a vulture." Tears brimmed in her eyes and her stomach clinched tight to suppress the nausea. "Get the hell out of my sight!" Her voice was cold and exact.

"Kasey," he began, but she stood up and turned her back to him in dismissal. "Your boyfriend hasn't been exactly honest with you either. You might want to ask him about that. Ask him who his father is." Neal tossed this directive over his shoulder as he left the building.

"I know about him being illegitimate," she retaliated. But Neal was already gone. At least Cort had been honest with her.

Kasey put her head down on the desk again. "What next?" she muttered. "What am I going to do now?"

Josh came back into the office from the warehouse after hearing Neal drive off. "Hey, Kase, what's wrong?" He hurried around the desk and put his arm around her when he saw the look on her face. "What's happened?"

"Did you know my father had borrowed money against the business?"

Josh propped on the edge of the desk and hesitated before answering. He wasn't sure if he should tell her the truth or not, but then, hadn't her father's death released him from his promise not to tell? And now Neal had spilled the beans.

"Josh?"

"Yes, Kase, I knew. Your father made me promise not to tell you. He was trying to take care of it before you found out. I was afraid that greedy bastard would be circling, but I had hopes of intervening." His grey eyes narrowed and hardened as he glanced across the parking lot at the disappearing car.

Josh changed the subject. "I just contacted one of our old clients and talked him into giving us some business again. He was a little hesitant, given our streak of bad luck, but he had some cargo that needed to go out right away and we were his only choice at the moment. Maybe we can convince him to bring his business back. We'll get there, don't give up."

"Yeah, but will that business be for us or for Neal Harrison?" Kasey put her hand on Josh's shoulder and squeezed affectionately.

"Why don't you get out of here and do something good for yourself? Victor and I can handle things." Josh inclined his head waiting for an answer.

"Is Victor here?"

"Yeah, he came in a few minutes ago. He wants to stay here through the night and make sure the place is safe. He blames himself for the ladder rung being cut. He says if he hadn't moved into his own place, the accident wouldn't have happened."

"Nonsense. Where is he now?"

"In the hangar."

Kasey went to find Victor. She had to convince him he wasn't at fault for the accident and talk him out of staying overnight. She didn't want anyone else hurt.

"It's okay. I'll be all right," Victor assured her, "and I've been thinking I might just move into that back room again, anyway. I can save some money that way."

"I don't know, Victor, I don't want you to do this. I mean, I don't want you to put your life at risk."

"Don't you worry your pretty little head. I am very aware of what I can and can't do, and besides, I have this," Victor lowered his voice and looked around before he withdrew a gun from his satchel.

"*What*? Where did you get *that*?" Kasey questioned. "Nothing good can come from having a gun."

"Like I said, don't worry your pretty little head. I know how to use this and I will be extra careful."

"We'll talk about this later." Kasey knew it would do her no good to protest any further. She wasn't totally convinced that it was a bad idea, either. First there was her father's "accident", then her own emergency landing, Josh's near fatal fall and Mr. McNamara's murder. Victor certainly had a right to protect himself. Especially since they were no closer to finding out who was responsible.

"Looks like you and Josh have things pretty well under control for now. I think I'll go home for a while and get something to eat. I can't stand any more bad news today." Kasey told Victor about the apparent murder at the Cordova Inn and also Neal's bombshell.

"So the gun isn't a bad idea with all that going on and like I told you before, that Harrison fellow and the cowboy are up to no good. I wish you would just stay away from them." There was a critical tone to his voice.

"Maybe the Harrison fellow, Victor, but the cowboy isn't all that thrilled with Neal, either, so he can't be all that bad. Maybe you're right about the gun. It's just that they make me nervous. Please be careful." Kasey sighed. "See you later."

Kasey had pulled into the stream of traffic and was headed for her apartment when suddenly a horrible thought occurred to her. What if she and Neal both had been the target in the plane crash? And what if Josh had been the person who sabotaged the plane? *That's crazy, but*—She tried to shrug the thought off.

Josh knew about mechanics, he had opportunities galore, and he would benefit with me and Neal out of the way. Pop and I both left the business to Josh in our wills. He would stand to inherit the business since I have no living relatives, at least none that I know about.

If Neal were out of the way Josh wouldn't have to pay back that large loan. But then, he had fallen from the ladder someone had sabotaged. Of course, that could've been to remove himself from suspicion. He wasn't injured very badly. No, he was too much like a brother; I won't consider him a suspect. Did Lieutenant Blanchard find out about the loan in his investigations? Does he consider Josh a suspect?

As terrible as it was, she had to consider *all* the people in her life who had motives. It was time for her to remove her head from the sand and take an active part in finding who was responsible for all this bad luck.

Cort pulled into the parking lot of the motel again and found the lieutenant waiting for him. He had called Blanchard and asked to meet with him before he left town. Blanchard motioned him to the parking space near him.

"You said earlier that you had some questions. What was it you wanted to talk to me about, Lieutenant?" Cort asked, his jaw clenched and his eyes slightly narrowed.

"How well did you know this Red McNamara?"

"What makes you think I knew him?" Cort countered.

"I found out recently that you met with him in Colorado a short time after Miss O'Brien's plane narrowly missed crashing at your ranch. Right after that he deposited five hundred dollars in his bank account." Blanchard watched Cort's expression carefully. "And you spoke with him by phone on more than one occasion, the last time being after he checked into the motel. Did you visit him here today before you went to Kasey's?"

"What are you getting at, Lieutenant? Do you think I had something to do with his death?"

"Did you?"

"No," Cort stated firmly.

"You didn't answer my other question. Were you here today, this morning? Was he your early appointment?"

"No, he was not my early appointment."

"Are you going to tell me what you're connection with Mr. McNamara is?"

"Not right now," Cort said smoothly, with no expression on his face.

Blanchard retained his easy manner, but there was a distinct hardening of his eyes. "I can't make you answer that question now, but I might warn you that you are rapidly moving up on the list of suspects." Blanchard turned to leave. He glanced at Cort's suitcase in the back seat. "I can reach you at the ranch if I have any further questions?"

Cort nodded. "I was on my way to the airport when I called you. I'll be back, though, in a few days." Cort pushed back his hat. "Do I need an attorney, Lieutenant?"

"To use your words, not right now. By the way, we had a long talk with Spencer Harrison. After some prodding he filled us in on your background. That doesn't look too good for you either in all this mess, seeing as how your half-brother was on board the plane with Miss O'Brien during the emergency landing."

A swift shadow of anger swept across Cort's face. "What do you mean by that remark?"

"Well, if Neal Harrison is out of the way you stand to inherit quite a tidy sum when the old man dies."

Cort stiffened at the suggestion. "From this point on, Lieutenant, all your questions should be directed to my attorney." Cort took out his wallet and thumbed through the contents. "Here's his card. Now, unless you intend to arrest me, our conversation has ended." Cort turned to leave then said, "I trust you will keep my private matters private, Lieutenant."

"For the time being."

Angrily, Cort put his rental car in gear and sped off. This conversation with Blanchard really threw a wrench into things. He couldn't blame his grandfather for telling the truth about him, though. It was only a matter of time before it was uncovered. Most people who were close to the family knew about it anyway.

Cort had made Neal and Spence swear they would keep the information in the family. It was no one else's business, especially if his own father wouldn't acknowledge him. Now he would be forced to tell Kasey before she found out another way. But first he had something more important to take care of.

Chapter Twelve

A shrill ringing sound broke sharply into Kasey's sleep and it took her a minute to determine it wasn't part of her dream. *It must be Cort letting me know he made it safely home.* Smiling lazily, she reached for the phone.

"Kasey, I think you'd better get down here to your office."

"Why? What's happened?" The tone in Blanchard's voice caused Kasey to sit straight up in bed.

"Victor surprised someone breaking into the office and he's been shot. It's just a flesh wound in the leg, but he's at the emergency room being patched up. I need you to come down here and tell me if anything is missing." Blanchard seemed distracted for the moment, then added, "We found marks on the door where the person forced the lock open."

"I'll be right there." Kasey depressed the button on the phone then dialed the hospital. Since it was only a short time ago that Josh was there, she still had the number on a pad by her phone. "Emergency room, please. Hello, can I speak to Victor Martin? He was brought in a short time ago with a gunshot wound. Yes, I'll hold."

Kasey stripped off her nightshirt and went to her closet. She pulled out a sweat suit and began dressing one-handed. Jumping around, she succeeded in getting one foot then the other into the pants. She managed to pull the sweat shirt over her head, but Kasey had one arm through the sleeve, about to switch the phone to her other hand, when Victor came on the line. She was so relieved to hear his voice. "Oh, Victor! Are you all right?"

"I'll be okay. Nothing more than a scratch, I promise. I'm a big boy and can handle this. Don't you worry none. I gotta go now, they're going to sew me up. I'll talk to you later."

There was hardly any traffic at one o'clock in the morning and Kasey arrived at her office in record time. Blanchard opened the car door for her.

"You didn't waste any time getting here, Kasey. I hope you didn't break any speed laws." He smiled, trying to put her at ease. "This may be just what it appears, an attempted burglary, and have nothing to do with the other episodes."

"At this point, Lieutenant, I don't believe anything that happens is a random act. I think I'm going to give my employees a vacation. This just proves what I thought earlier. I can't justify risking anyone else's life in the name of saving my business. But I'll be damned if I'm going to roll over and play dead, either."

Kasey took a deep ragged breath. She was tired, tired of the stress, tired of the continued attacks, and for what? Neal was going to get Cimmaron Air anyway, because her father didn't have anything else worth the kind of money he owed. One thing was certain, she was going to find out who killed her father, who possibly tried to kill her, and *why*.

"Do you have any ideas at all who might be responsible for all this? For Pop's murder?" Kasey asked as she walked into the hangar with Lt. Blanchard.

"We have several very good leads and I can almost promise you an arrest will be made soon."

"Can I ask who you have in mind?"

"I'm afraid I'm not at liberty to say just yet, but it will be soon." The lieutenant put his hand on her shoulder. "And I think that it's an excellent idea to close shop for the time being."

"I didn't say anything about closing the shop, Lieutenant."

Blanchard leaned closer to Kasey and looked directly into her eyes. "You're not thinking about running the air business all by yourself?"

"Lieutenant!" a deputy called out. "We need you over here for a minute."

"Excuse me, Kasey. Don't leave. I want to talk to you about this hare- brained idea you have. Check for missing items," he reminded her.

"Sure, I'll just look around. About the only thing anyone could take would be in the office. I don't see any of our equipment missing out here. We don't keep money or checks in the office, that is, when we have them, but we have computers and calculators—" Suddenly she remembered something from the last incident. It came out of nowhere. She followed Blanchard into the office.

"Lieutenant, remember when Josh fell from the ladder? Well, when I got here that day, Morley Forbes was sitting in the office. I don't know how long he had been here. Also, I wouldn't put it past him to have been involved in the oil line being cut. He has a key and access to the planes, as well as the building. He was out of town when Pop left here but he could've been the one who met him."

"What motive would he have?"

"I don't know, but then what motive would anyone have?"

"I'll talk to Josh and find out if Forbes was here when he arrived and I'll check on his whereabouts when your father left. Thanks, Kasey."

Kasey walked around the desk and immediately saw the blood on the floor. Pinpoints of lights blurred her vision and the next thing she knew someone was gently slapping her wrists and calling her name.

Victor had been released from the hospital and was recuperating at home. Kasey was glad she had convinced him to keep his apartment instead of moving back into the warehouse. She tried to talk him out of going back to the office until this business was over and the police had the guilty party in custody, but she knew he would not take her advice on this. She hadn't heard from Josh for a couple of days, but knew he was out somewhere still trying to solicit business.

Both Josh and Victor were firmly against closing Cimmaron Air. They made a good case, stating that whoever was behind all the "accidents" would win if they were trying to put them out of business. If another murder had been the motive, then the perpetrator's attempts were not successful. He was getting sloppy.

Lieutenant Blanchard knocked on the door and glanced around the area. The apartment was in a lower-income neighborhood with partially dismantled cars at the curb or in yards. Children played noisily in the street, breaking up their games when a car entered their makeshift playground.

When there was no answer, Blanchard knocked harder. There was a sudden movement near the window covering, then the sound of two locks being turned. The door opened a crack and when the occupant saw who was there, it opened wider.

"Lieutenant, what can I do for you?"

"I need to ask you a couple of questions, Victor. Do you mind if I come in? I'll only be a minute or two."

"No. Don't mind the mess. I haven't been keeping up with my housekeeping chores lately." Victor stepped aside and allowed Blanchard to enter.

"I was wondering if you could give me a description of the person who shot you."

"Actually, Lieutenant, it was dark and I really couldn't see the man too clearly. I was sleeping in the back room and I heard a noise. I guess that was when he broke in."

"How tall was he? Was he slim, heavy set?"

Victor rubbed his chin and thought for a minute. "I guess he was about my height, six feet, maybe a little taller. He was muscular or he never would've gotten the drop on me."

"After he shot you he just left without taking anything?"

"I suppose he figured someone might've heard the shot and come running."

"The nearest building was yards away and there is noise from airplanes taking off."

"There isn't much air traffic at midnight, Lieutenant, and there is a security guard that drives around. How the hell should I know what this bastard was thinking?"

"Sorry, Victor. I have to ask these questions." Blanchard walked to the door. His hand was on the knob when he turned back to Victor. "We collected the bullet and if we find the gun, maybe we can trace it back to him. If you think of anything else, please call me. I hope your leg gets better soon."

"Lieutenant, I didn't get a chance to tell you since they rushed me off to the hospital and all. The man shot me with my own gun. He took it away from me in the struggle. Kasey told me nothing good could come from having the gun. She was right."

"Is there anything else you neglected to tell me?"

"Nope, that's about it."

"I'll need to have the paperwork on that gun."

Victor looked down at the floor. "Don't have any. I bought the gun from a man I met when I was hitching out here. It was for protection. Am I going to be in trouble?"

"I'll let you know," Blanchard answered angrily and he walked out the door.

Kasey was too restless just sitting around her apartment, so she decided to go to the office and catch up on some paperwork. She was just about to leave when a knock sounded at her door.

"Lieutenant. What's up?"

"Mind if I come in?"

"Not at all. Do you have some news for me?"

"Not yet. I just have a question for you. How well do you know that guy, and his family, Kasey?"

"Which guy are you talking about?"

"Cort Navarro."

"I know him pretty well but I don't know much about his family. They are somewhere in Mexico and Cort says he has never seen them."

"You spent some time at his grandfather's ranch, isn't that right?"

"I spent a few days at the Harrisons' ranch. *Neal's* grandfather's ranch."

"Well, in a way it's partly Navarro's as well. He stands to inherit some of it when the old man dies."

"I knew Cort and Spence were close but I didn't realize it was *that* close a relationship."

"Hasn't Navarro told you yet that he's also Spencer Harrison's grandson—Neal Harrison's half-brother?"

Kasey was too stunned to answer for a moment, but didn't want Blanchard to know how hard the news had hit her. She shook her head. "I'm sorry Lieutenant, I was just on my way out. Was there anything else?"

"No. I'm just following up on some leads. I guess I should have called, but I was in the neighborhood anyway." Blanchard hadn't told her the whole truth. He was hoping Cort Navarro might have beat it down here after his phone call to the ranch.

"When I hear from Cort, though, I'll let him know you were asking about him."

Kasey closed the door and slumped against it. *Why didn't Cort tell me, why was this a big secret? Spence, Neal, they had plenty of opportunities and yet they never mentioned —wait, Spence said something. What was it? I know. It was the day I left. He said something about wanting me to become a member of the family and when I said Neal wasn't my type he answered —what? Something about his grandson—Was he trying to tell me then about Cort?* She needed to talk to Cort and get answers. Another thought entered her mind. This one was chilling.

*What if Neal had actually been the target all along and Cort was responsible? He would then have a larger inheritance— But what about the attempt on Josh's life and Victor's gunshot wound—maybe to conceal the identity of the true victim, Neal Harrison? But then maybe the true victim was Cimmaron Air. Was someone trying to ruin the charter service? Why, why, **why**?* So many questions popped into her head and so many emotions washed over her.

Kasey shook her mind free of the thoughts, picked up her briefcase and left her apartment. She would deal with all that later when her head was clear. Right now she was angry, hurt and confused.

When she drove onto the parking lot, Kasey saw an unfamiliar car. Thinking it might be a new client, she glanced in the mirror and checked her hair, then put a quick touch-up to her lipstick, but when she entered the office, it was Spence she found there. He was standing in the office door looking into the hangar, his back to her.

"Spence! What are you doing here?"

He took one look at her and knew all was not right. "You don't seem too happy to see me. Something wrong, Kasey?"

"You might say that. I was just told some really disturbing news. I want to know why it came from someone other than Cort?"

"I'm not sure I can answer for Cort but if you tell me what, I might know something about it."

"Why did none of you tell me Cort was your grandson?" There was silence. "Spence?"

"Blanchard told me he was going to spill the beans about Cort, so I beat it down here. I couldn't take a chance on Cort getting back in time to tell you himself and I was hoping to be ahead of him." Spence took a seat in front of her desk. "I'm sorry, Kasey, but it was at Cort's request and I wouldn't go against his wishes. I hope you'll forgive me, but he had his reasons."

"I'd like to talk to him about this."

"He's not where I can reach him and it might be couple of days before I'll be able to. I'll have him call you." Spence was silent again, searching for something more to say. "Forgive me, Kasey?"

"How did he come to the ranch? I know his mother died after his birth and, from what I gather, his father wasn't there. How did Cort's father meet his mother, since she never came to the States? If it's too personal —"

"I'll skip the personal stuff." Spence took a deep breath, his voice resigned. "My son, Raymond, went to college with Liliana's brother, Jorge. One summer Ray went to Mexico with Jorge and that's how he met her. Liliana was Cort's mother. She was only sixteen, seventeen when she gave birth, just a baby herself.

"I didn't know about Liliana and the baby until Consuelo had a priest write me a letter. By the time I got there it was too late, of course." When he spoke again his voice was heavy with sarcasm. "It seems no one could locate Ray. When I arrived Liliana was dead and Consuelo was caring for my grandson in a small house badly in need of a lot of work and with basically no money. They would have been on the streets starving, except for the generosity of the church. Cort was of my blood! I couldn't leave him or Consuelo like that, so I filled out all the papers needed to bring them home with me."

Spence sighed heavily. Visiting old memories left him tired and unsettled. He mentally relived the terrible argument with his son and the subsequent long estrangement. It was only after Neal was born three years later that Ray finally got in touch. Now, the only time Spence saw Ray was when they were in L.A. at the same time. Ray refused to come to the ranch as long as Cort, was there.

"I'm sorry, Spence. I'm not angry with you. Right now I am at odds with *both* your grandsons, but I'll deal with them." Kasey had one more question, "I know how difficult it must be for you, with your emotions torn between father and son. Do you think Cort and his father will ever get together?"

"Who's to say? I believe in miracles, and before I die I would like for that one to come to pass. I hope that Ray will come to his senses and beg Cort's forgiveness. He's missed so much. He has a wonderful son in Cort, one that he could be very proud of."

As an afterthought Kasey noted, "You said Cort was away. He sure travels a lot for a ranch foreman. Is that common?"

Spence looked as if he were weighing the question before he answered. "Sometimes." To avoid further discussion, he added, "Now, how about lunch? My treat."

Chapter Thirteen

Cort entered the small cafe and nodded at the blonde waitress. He sat down at the counter and picked up the plastic-coated menu.

"Hey, Cowboy, where've you been? Haven't seen you in here lately."

"Around. You have a good memory."

"I don't forget something like you." She smiled seductively and smoothed her uniform down over her hips. "What can I get for you?"

He glanced around the room, noting the increase in diners since his previous trip and thought the blonde might have something to do with that. "What's good?"

"Well, I can take that two ways." She watched for his reaction.

Cort smiled. "From the menu."

"Ah, still playing hard to get. Okay, but I don't give up easily." She smiled back at him and held a pen poised above the order slip. "The Yankee pot roast is good, but stay away from the meatloaf."

"I'll take the pot roast." He closed the menu and put it back in the provided metal stand. "By the way, how long have you worked here?"

"Eight or nine months. Why?"

"I had a friend stop in here about a year ago and he was telling me about this remarkable waitress in her seventies. I didn't see her when I was in before and it doesn't look like she's here today."

"Oh, that was Ethel. I'm just as good, maybe even better," she said, a hand on her hip and a pout on her face.

"Where is Ethel? Did she retire?"

The blonde shrugged her shoulders and considered her answer. "She and the cook disappeared one afternoon and never showed up again." She glanced uneasily over her shoulder and shifted her weight from one foot to the other.

"Has anybody bothered to find out what happened to them?"

"You'd best talk to the sheriff about that." Her answer was abrupt and her manner had changed completely. "I'll get your order." She turned and walked quickly around the corner and pushed through double doors.

Cort watched through the pass-through window as she entered the kitchen and leaned close to the cook, whispering in his ear. Both turned and looked at Cort suspiciously.

The cook went to the wall and picked up the phone. Within five minutes a police officer strolled through the door. He walked to the counter and sat down next to Cort.

"I hear you're looking for someone."

"Is that a crime?"

"It might be, seeing as how the person you're looking for was murdered."

Cort was caught off guard by the answer, but he held his emotions in check. "And the cook?"

"I think you'd best come to the office with me. I'd like to find out what your interest is in all this."

"Am I under arrest?"

"That depends. Now if you'll just come with me quietly, we can get this over with."

The next morning on her way to work, Kasey stopped by a walk-in salon to get her hair cut. It was less expensive and she didn't need an appointment. Events in her life kept postponing the endeavor and now she had put it off long enough. Twenty minutes later she was on her way to the office feeling much lighter.

As she drove, her mind addressed the criminal acts against her and her crew and who could be responsible. Lieutenant Blanchard hadn't filled her in on his possible suspects yet and the motive was still a mystery. She absolutely refused to believe one of her friends was responsible. Kasey had known Norm for a long time; he had been in high school with her in Van Nuys. Josh? No, she wouldn't consider him. Besides he had worked with Cimmaron Air for five years, why would he suddenly start sabotaging the business? What would be his motive? Victor was her knight in shining armor and he had been made a victim as had been Josh. Norm and Alice were the only ones not drawn into this mystery.

Then there was Forbes. He had made a number of threats. Could he possibly be making good on them? What was his motive? Kasey wasn't conceited enough to think it was because she had spurned his romantic advances. So what then?

Learning about Cort and his parentage made Kasey realize he might have a very big motive. Not only that, but he was away on business an inordinate amount of time for a foreman. What business could he have that required so much attention away from the ranch? And where did he go? He came here a few times. Cort was in town when Arthur McNamara was killed—

Kasey shook her head to clear the disturbing thoughts about Cort. How could she be drawn to someone involved in criminal activity? *Fool, it happens all the time. Affairs of the heart leave you open to be blindsided. So what am I missing?*

A small jet flew low over her car, bringing Kasey's attention back to her driving. She had almost driven right past the road into the airport while she was distracted.

Neal drove onto the parking lot of Cimmaron Air the same time as Kasey.

He opened her car door and offered a hand to help her out. She refused his assistance, grabbing her briefcase and getting out of the car under her own steam.

"Neal. Another visit?" She managed to comment through stiff lips.

"Hello, Kasey. I need to talk to you."

"So talk."

"Can we go inside? I'm here on rather distasteful business." Neal's tone was apologetic and his eyes darted back and forth between her and the building.

"And why should I think any differently?" She dropped her car keys in the side compartment of her purse and walked toward the office. Neal was ahead of her and opened the door to allow her to enter.

"Have a seat. I'll be with you in just a minute." Kasey put her purse and briefcase down and crossed to the hangar door. Opening it, she saw Victor helping Josh unload freight from the Six. She was pleased the order had come in.

Kasey poured herself a cup of coffee, purposely not offering one to Neal. She took a sip before speaking again. "Now, what can I do for you?" She took a seat behind her desk.

"I have the authority as a process server to serve these papers. I've placed a lien on the planes and equipment and this is the hearing regarding my taking over the property, unless you can come up with the—" Neal glanced at the paperwork he was holding, "He paid me seven thousand dollars. That leaves a one hundred and ninety-two thousand five hundred dollar balance."

Kasey sat staring at the paperwork, shock causing any words to wedge in her throat. When she was finally able to speak, she chose what she had to say carefully. Now was not the time to lose her temper and make matters worse.

"Wait, you said he borrowed one hundred and fifty thousand dollars!"

"There was interest accruing over the last eighteen months. When I loan money out, I'm losing interest on it and I'm in this business to make money, my dear."

Clenching her teeth, she was furious. "You know I don't have that kind of money. If you take the planes, I'm out of business. Give me a few days to try and get financing."

"This is going to sound cruel, but it's fact. No one is going to finance a company with such a poor track record. They'll take one look at the accidents and your father flying into a mountain—Wait." He held up a hand. "Let me finish. Yes, it appears your father was murdered, but that hasn't been proven yet and no arrests have been made."

"So you're going to close us up, just like that."

"If you'll notice there is a court date on that paper. After the hearing you and your crew are welcome to stay on and run the business for me."

"That's mighty big-hearted of you. Are you sure you want to take the risk, what with our 'poor track record' and 'all the accidents'?" Kasey stared at Neal mockingly. "You can take your job offer and shove it up your ass." She stomped out of the office and went straight to Josh.

"I guess the buzzard has stopped circling and come down to tear the flesh off the carcass. What are you planning to do?" Josh removed his hat and scratched his head.

"Regardless of what he said, I'm still going to try to get some financing. One hundred and ninety-two thousand, five hundred dollars is a lot of money, but the two new clients you got and the ones we already have, maybe will have some sway."

"I'll see what I can come up with, too. How much time is he giving you?"

"I'm not sure. I kinda flew off the handle and came in here to cool down. Now, I gotta go back and see what I can do." Her eyes were filled with contempt as she watched Neal going through his paperwork in her office.

"You say he wants one hundred and ninety-two thousand, five hundred dollars? That's a lot of dough."

Kasey turned and stared at Josh. "I won't accept defeat, not before I've tried everything I can think of." Kasey took deep breaths to calm down. She was really angry with her father right now for getting them into so much debt. *For the life of me, I can't figure out where all that money went. Yes, Pop had paid some back, but still there should be money on the books.*

There was rent, utilities, gas, supplies, and payroll. They each took a salary for living expenses. Alice was paid a small salary to take care of the office and there was an occasional fee for Norm Lang when they needed an extra pilot.

Granted, those operating expenses ate into the hundred and fifty thousand, but not enough to deplete that amount in the short time between borrowing it and flying into a mountainside. They did have some money coming in, too. She had to see how much money they really had and go from there.

Neal could see Kasey and Josh through the office door. He watched them talking, trying to determine the tone of the conversation from their body language. Kasey, he knew, was agitated, but he couldn't pinpoint Josh's take on the news. Noticing that Kasey was returning to the office, Neal turned back around and shuffled through the papers in front of him.

"How much time can you give me?" she asked, stepping around the desk and sitting down.

"Kasey," he began, but she interrupted him.

"Look, you — Neal, this business was a dream of my father's. He worked damned hard to realize it. I won't turn it over to you without a fight." She held up a hand to stop him when he started to speak as he had done to her earlier. "I know, you have the law on your side, but the least you can do is give me a chance. That's all I'm asking for—a chance."

Neal considered the situation and Kasey held her breath. He picked up the remaining papers and put them back in his briefcase.

"One week, Kasey. That's it. If you can come up with the money, then I'll request a dismissal of the hearing. The payments are a year in arrears and I haven't done anything about it because of the accident and investigations. Now that your father has been declared dead, I have to."

"What if I can come up with most of it, will you let me make payments on the rest?"

"No. It's all or nothing." He snapped the case shut and stood up. "It's not like I get a cheap thrill from all this. It's business. And my business—"

"Is to make money." Kasey finished his sentence, mimicking his statement from earlier.

The next few days Kasey went to several different lending institutions, only to be turned down by all of them. None gave her a reason, just the standard rejection.

"What are we going to do, Kase? I've tried to get money, too, and no luck. After the next two shipments, we don't even have any new prospects," Josh said.

"I'll have to cut back as much as possible. What else can I do? As bad as I hate it, I'm going to have to let Alice and Norm go. I don't like to think about it, but you and Victor might have to go to work for someone else. I'll get by on as little as I can."

"We'll face that when we come to it."

"In the meantime, I'll keep searching the paperwork here in the office. Maybe I can find the missing funds."

"Mind if I disappear for a couple hours? I need to take care of something. By the way, there's a small package I brought in.

The guy wants it delivered to his office by four o'clock. The address is on the packing slip."

"You don't have to ask. Go. Get out of here. I'll see the package gets delivered."

Kasey rubbed her eyes. So many numbers and still they didn't add up to the missing amount. She got up and went back to the filing cabinet, replacing the paperwork she had withdrawn earlier and pulled out more. She was about to shove the drawer in when she noticed the grey tip of a book sticking out from the back edge. She laid the papers down in a chair beside the cabinet and tried pulling the drawer out further. Something was stopping it and she thought it might be the book.

Reaching in as far as she could, Kasey pulled on the object until it finally gave and she almost toppled backward. There was a soft thud indicating something had also dropped behind the drawers. She wasn't sure what it was but decided to check out the book first, then find whatever had fallen.

Kasey took the long slender book to her desk and opened it. Seven entries consisting of dates beside which were numbers, lined the page. She recognized her father's writing. The entries stopped two days before his death. She added the numbers. Of the one hundred and fifty thousand dollars Neal said he had loaned to her father, Patrick had transferred twenty-three thousand dollars to the regular business ledger. Kasey had seen that entry and really hadn't questioned a twenty-three thousand dollar income, assuming her father had consolidated payments from a few jobs. The checks Alice gave her to sign had used up that amount and more in the year since her father died. That explained how the bills were at least being paid.

Twenty thousand more went to a private investigator, which her father noted was "up front" money. The following five months of his life he paid the same man four thousand a month. In parenthesis her father scribbled the note, "keeps coming back for more money. When will it end?" That totaled sixty-three thousand dollars.

The last entry was for seven thousand dollars paid to Neal, bringing the grand total to seventy thousand dollars spent. That left eighty thousand dollars. If she could find that money maybe she could use it to bargain with Neal.

She pulled out her planner and thumbed through the business cards until she found Neal's. Kasey dialed his number and got voice mail. She was hesitant about leaving a message, but wanted to get this cleared up.

"I've been going over my father's accounts and have a question about the loan. Please call me at your earliest convenience."

"Hi Kasey. Sorry about the voice mail. I was on another call." Neal came on the line just as she was hanging up. "What's the problem?"

"What was the percentage rate on the loan?"

"Twenty-two percent. Kasey dear, It's business and I have to charge interest. Any place you borrow money you have to pay interest."

Kasey smacked herself in the forehead. *Of course! How stupid of me. I just used up most of my brainpower trying to make all the totals jibe. I hate math and anything to do with it.* "What percent?"

"Twenty-two."

"That's rather steep, isn't it? I mean, I'm not up on the going interest rates, but that seems damn high to me."

"You forget, Kasey, my loans hold a certain level of risk. Most of the folks who come to me aren't able to take out a conventional loan. Anyway, some of your credit card companies charge twenty-two percent. I think I'm fair, considering." Neal was silent a minute, then asked, "Are you saying you have the money for me?"

"No, Neal. I'm just doing some house cleaning." She bit down hard on her lower lip. "You wouldn't consider lowering the interest amount?"

"Or you offering me something in return?" Neal laughed into the phone. "Sorry, Lady Ace, no can do. Don't forget the hearing at one o'clock today."

Kasey slammed the phone down, fury almost choking her. She dropped her head into her hands and waited for the anger to pass. Anger certainly wouldn't help matters any. And besides she wanted to get away from the stress for a while. Closing the ledgers, she stood up to return them to the file cabinet when she remembered the object that had fallen behind the cabinet. Kasey put the books back on the desk and searched through the drawers for a flashlight.

She removed the file drawer and got on her knees, shining the light towards the back of the cabinet. Because it was the same color and lay at an odd angle, she almost missed the small wooden box. She pulled it out and placed it on the desk.

"Kasey, I just put that package to Carrollton Engineering in your car so you can deliver it after the hearing. That way you won't have to come back here for it."

Kasey glanced up from her desk. "Oh, you startled me, I didn't see you come in. All these figures and still no trace of the missing money."

"Sorry, I can't help you there." Victor glanced at the clock.

"I know, I know. I'm leaving. You gonna be here for a while?"

"No, I'm leaving pretty soon, too. Josh is supposed to be back and I thought I'd leave then. Did you need me to stay?"

Kasey shook her head. "Just lock up if Josh hasn't returned when you're ready to leave. I have to come back later anyway and finish up some things around here." She stood up, arching her back with her elbows pulled behind her to relieve the ache between her shoulder blades.

"What were you getting out of the cabinet?"

"I'm not sure what it is but I don't have time to mess with it now. Must be something of Pop's." She placed the box in her bag and returned the ledgers to the file drawer.

Hearing the sound of a car, Victor looked out the front window. "Looks like you're not going to get out of here after all. I see Forbes driving in."

"Oh, hell. I'm going out through the hangar. Do me a big favor and keep him talking until I can get in my car and leave. I can't handle a confrontation with him right now."

Kasey picked up her briefcase and purse and hurried into the hangar. She waited until Forbes was out of his car and entering the office before making a beeline to her car. When she looked into the rear view mirror, he was rushing outside waving papers in the air and yelling at her. When Kasey failed to stop the car, he flipped her off.

"I'm through with you, missy! You just put the nail in your coffin!"

Kasey fought her way through the noonday traffic, one eye on the street ahead and one on her dashboard clock. She wanted to get to the court in plenty of time for the hearing. Maybe she could get an extension. Suddenly a car pulled out from the side street in front of her and she slammed on her brakes. The car behind her didn't have time to stop and he careened into the other lane but not before he clipped her bumper.

"Not now! I don't have time for this." Kasey moaned as she exited her vehicle to inspect the damage.

"Are you all right?" Kasey asked as the man got out of his car.

"Yes. Are you?"

"I'm fine and it looks like I only have a scratch on my bumper. Your headlight appears to be broken out and there's some minor damage on your fender."

After they exchanged the needed information, Kasey removed a small camera from her purse and took pictures. Noticing two men on the sidewalk watching the scene, she hurried over and asked if they had witnessed the accident. Both agreed they had and she wrote down their name and phone numbers in case she needed them at a future date. She had learned to cover herself.

In California one didn't need to call the police on a fender bender, but did need to fill out an accident report and turn it into the Department of Motor Vehicles. This would definitely save time. Kasey was barely going to make it to court as it was.

Everything was going against her. After the accident there was a heavy traffic delay and by the time Kasey got to the courthouse she was at a run. Hurrying down the hallway, she made note of each courtroom until she came to the appointed one. When she opened the door, the room was empty. Her heart sank.

For a moment Kasey stood in the doorway not sure what to do next. The door in the back opened and a young woman came out and picked up some paperwork from the desk beside the judge's bench.

"Miss, I'm here for a hearing that was scheduled at one o'clock. Can you tell me what happened?"

"Harrison versus O'Brien?"

"Yes, Ma'am."

"I have the paperwork here. If you'll come down I'll give you your copy. Kasey O'Brien, right?"

Kasey nodded. She tried to force her emotions into order. Fear caused her hand to tremble when she took the papers from the clerk. She wouldn't look at them now—she'd do that later, alone in her apartment when there would be no one to observe her reaction. The outcome was pretty obvious since she had missed her court appointment.

Kasey felt a nauseating sinking of despair as she read through the document. Her father's hard work building the business was all for naught. Cimmaron Air now belonged to Neal Harrison. He would likely sell it and the planes for the money owed him. She paced the floor, her arms wrapped around her middle. What was she to do now?

Tossing the papers on the couch, Kasey caught a glimpse of the small box she found in the file cabinet earlier. Hoping an answer of some sort might be in its contents, she took it to the dining room table and opened it. A bunch of yellowed newspaper clippings were folded neatly and stacked inside.

A box of keepsakes. Kasey smiled. She wasn't aware her father saved memorabilia from the past. He had never mentioned it. In fact, they never talked about the past. Funny, she had never really thought about the past for a long time and then only as a mild curiosity.

Carefully she placed the first clipping on her table and smoothed out the page. The news clipping was from the <u>Akron Beacon Journal</u>, dated June 6, 1983.

KIDNAPPING, DRUGS AND MURDER

Trial begins today in the kidnapping and murder charge against Mallory Richards of Akron Air Charter Service. Richards is accused of kidnapping Frances and Kasey O'Brien, the wife and daughter of Patrick O'Brien, his partner and fellow Marine.

Presumably O'Brien stumbled onto a large shipment of cocaine flown in from Mexico by Richards. To keep his partner from reporting him, Richards kidnapped O'Brien's family.

While being held captive, Frances O'Brien came down with pneumonia, and this resulted in her death.

Kasey sat stunned. *Why had Pop never talked about this? Why don't I remember?* She studied the three grainy photographs above the article. One was Patrick holding five year-old Kasey's hand in front of a courthouse. Another was the image of her mother. She ran her fingers lovingly over the picture. Not remembering what her mother looked like, Kasey was surprised to see how much she resembled the young woman in the photograph.

As she examined the clipping a memory suddenly flashed in her mind. It was a memory she had experienced before—at the ranch. The rainstorm and the cabin had brought it on but she couldn't remember it after she regained consciousness. Now it was there again. She was certain it was the same thing her mind recalled that day. A child's cry and a dark, wet place. Was that her crying? There was something else. A woman moaned somewhere in the shadows.

Kasey closed her eyes and tried to concentrate. She heard sounds of water sloshing around as a dark figure came down the steps and walked towards her. She couldn't see his face, but it was definitely a man and fear rose in her throat until she couldn't make a sound. Then the memories faded and Kasey could not recall anything else. Picking up the news account again, she studied it more closely.

The third photograph was of the man accused of her mother's murder. Richards was depicted in handcuffs, being escorted by officers from a van to a building, presumably jail. His face was not clear enough for Kasey to make out his features.

As she continued to read the account, Kasey had a startling thought. Could this person, this Richards, be responsible for all the accidents and for killing her father? It would certainly make sense. Had he gotten out of prison recently? Had he even been convicted? Or maybe he hired someone while in prison to do his dirty work.

She checked the rest of the contents but found no more articles about the trial. Kasey decided to take this information to Lieutenant Blanchard and see if he could help her find out more, but she still had the package to deliver.

Kasey placed a call to Lieutenant Blanchard, but his line was busy. She would deliver the package and call him later and ask him to meet her at the office. Maybe there was more information behind the file cabinet and together they could go over all that she had found.

Chapter Fourteen

Cort leaned across the desk toward Blanchard. "I have someone for you to meet. He's a little shaky, so go easy on him." He motioned toward a man in his early forties, five feet six inches tall and balding. "Say hello to Frank Morgan."

Blanchard stood up and extended his hand. His eyes shifted from Cort to Morgan. "Hi, Frank. What can I do for you?"

"For years something has been hounding me, Lieutenant, and when Cort here found me, I figured it was time to talk."

Blanchard pulled up an extra chair and motioned for the man to sit down. "Please."

"About twenty-five years ago, I worked for Mallory Richards' Akron Air Service. I was young, a general flunky, but I learned a lot. Anyway, I had brought this twin-engine airplane in out of the weather —"

*   *   *   *   *   *   *   *

Akron, Ohio- June,1983

Dark clouds hovered overhead and it looked like there would be a cloudburst at any minute. Wind blew dirt across the tarmac and trees bent and swayed violently. The Piper

Navajo rocked in the wind as a small tug pulled it through tall doors. Two men in coveralls pulled the hangar doors shut behind the plane.

Patrick came through the office door into the hangar. He watched while TJ opened the cargo door and began to unload cartons marked MEDICAL EMERGENCY-HANDLE WITH CARE, setting them on a skid. After all four boxes were in place, TJ drove the forklift over and lifted the skid. The forks were too high and one hit the top carton, puncturing it. White powder slipped through the gash in the side. TJ backed up the forklift.

"Hey, TJ, hold on a minute," Patrick called out over the noise. The forklift stopped and the engine shut down. He hurried over to the torn carton and inspected the damage. "Got a knife?"

"No. I'll get one." TJ walked to the workbench and opened a drawer, pulling out a razor knife.

"Thanks." Patrick cut the tape and pried open the box. He removed the packing and lifted out a bag. Moving more quickly, his hands dug wildly through the box. His breath was shallow and quick, his face red. "What the hell is this?" He picked up a handful of powder and rubbed it between his finger and thumb.

"Damned sure ain't aspirin."

"What's on the manifest?"

TJ climbed into the Navajo, looked through the briefcase and brought out some papers. He gave them to Patrick who flipped through the papers finding one to his liking and read it, mumbling. He held the paper out with one hand and slapped it with the back of the other.

"This is the most stupid thing I've ever seen. We don't ship medical supplies *from* Mexico, we ship them *to* Mexico." He was furious and stomped to the phone on the wall, dialing a number with a shaking finger.

"Mallory, we need you down here—No, it can't wait!" He slammed the phone down.

Patrick, Mallory and TJ looked at the open box. "What do you mean you didn't know? You're the damned pilot. You're supposed to know what the hell cargo you're hauling."

"TJ, take the rest of the day off. Go home and enjoy that beautiful wife of yours. I'll let you know when to come back to work," Mallory said, placing his hand on TJ's shoulder.

TJ's eyes shifted from Mallory to Patrick. At Patrick's nod he left hastily, closing the door behind him.

*   *   *   *   *   *   *   *

Blanchard and Cort hung on every word. "I was more stupid than curious. Patrick was really pissed and I liked him a lot, so I thought I would hang around a little while to see what happened."

"Go on, go on," Blanchard prompted.

"I stopped at the door and listened."

*   *   *   *   *   *   *   *

"This is twice now. That's it. I'm calling the cops this time. I don't want to be taken down for some stupid ass thing you've done." Patrick went over to the phone and dialed 911. Mallory hurried through the office doors, reappearing with a chrome plated thirty-eight, sticking it under Patrick's chin.

"What's your emergency?" the dispatcher asked.

Mallory depressed the button. Patrick replaced the receiver and moved away from the phone. "You leave me no other choice. You've backed me into that old proverbial corner," Mallory told him through clenched teeth.

Patrick leaned against the wall sweating, Mallory's gun now pressed into his gut. He stared into the eyes of his friend and fellow Marine. He no longer recognized the man looking back at him.

"Stay there," Mallory ordered and picked up the phone with his left hand, dialing numbers. "Hi. Simon? Richards. Mallory Richards. It has come to fruition. You know what to do. Don't blow it." Mallory hung up the phone and looked at Patrick.

"What's the matter with you, Mallory? You used to be the greatest. *Semper Fi*. What happened?"

"I am great. It's just that I'm great at something different than what you expect. We all have our specialties—mine is making money. My wife piddles her money out to me like I was her damned kid. I need more."

"Who is Simon? What has come to fruition?"

"A plan, Patrick, a plan. I knew if you found out I was still in the 'import' business you would do just what you did. You're way too clean, way too clean. In an hour or so, Fran and Kasey will be hidden away. You have only one chance to ever see them again, so listen carefully."

Patrick lunged at Mallory's throat. Mallory shoved the gun into his gut again and cocked the hammer. "When Simon calls back, you will be free to go. Free to go anywhere as long as it's away from here. When I'm convinced you haven't gone to the cops, I will send your wife and kid to you. All you have to do is let me know where you are and that it's a very long way away."

"My God. How did you come to this?" Patrick stepped sideways, relieving the pressure of the gun. "If you hurt them I'll see you in hell."

Mallory had a wicked grin on his face. "I don't think you are in a place to make threats."

*   *   *   *   *   *   *   *

"I changed my name to Frank Morgan and my wife and I moved to California," Frank continued. "I was scared he'd come after us, too. After all, he knew I saw that cocaine was in the carton. Quite a bit of cocaine—worth millions."

Blanchard picked up his phone and dialed. "Hi, Cricket, Lieutenant Blanchard. Hey, can you do a quick work-up on a Mallory Richards? Yes, as soon as you can. Thanks."

By the time Kasey drove her car out of her apartment's parking garage and headed back to the office, it was five-thirty. There had only been time to grab something to eat and change into some sweats after the delivery. The weather had turned cooler and she wanted to wear something more substantial than the dress pants she had on.

Kasey had tried Blanchard's number again but he had someone in his office. This time she left her name and cell phone number and asked him to call her as soon as possible.

Dark clouds hovered in the sky causing it to appear much later in the evening. It had been some time since the last rainfall and, although it would be welcome, Kasey's fear of storms left her uneasy.

She drove north on Woodley toward Sherman Way, her thoughts on the latest events. It all seemed surreal to her. Kasey wondered how much time Neal would allow her to remove her personal items and wrap up unfinished business.

Now Cimmaron Air belonged to someone else and the idea was completely foreign to her. She had informed her employees she no longer needed them. The hardest one to let go was Alice, who had been like a mother to Kasey. Norm could get in touch with Neal for a job. Josh and Victor already had offers, but Alice was at an age employers hesitated to consider, even though it was against the law.

Kasey had driven by Alice's on her way home from the office. She chose this particular day to give her the bad news because it was Alice's day off. She didn't want to deliver the bad news at work. Kasey didn't want to deliver it at all, but in private was a much better choice.

She knocked on Alice's door. Kasey's misery was so acute it caused physical pain in her stomach. She heard the lock click and the door opened.

Alice took one look at her and took her by the arm, pulling her inside. "My goodness, honey. What's wrong?"

"Oh, Alice." The tears came freely now. "I—I have bad news. Please don't take it personally, because it's not. You probably already know since I had to cut your hours back so much—" Kasey was babbling, trying to get out what she had to say before she lost her nerve.

"There, there, dear. I suspected it was coming, I had just held out hope you would find some way to hang on." Alice took Kasey in her arms and held her close for a minute. "I can still come in and help you out and you don't have to pay me a thing. It's not like I depend on my salary there for a living. It's just getting out and doing something instead of sitting around here."

"I couldn't ask you to do that."

"I believe I was the one who suggested it."

"We don't have any business right now to even warrant you coming in."

"Well, you just let me know if you need me and I'll be right there."

The signal light changed and a car horn sounded from behind Kasey, bringing her back to the present. She wiped her eyes with the back of her hand and turned her attention to the traffic. She still had four more miles before she reached the airport.

Kasey pulled into a parking space beside Forbes' car. *Now is not the time for this.* She had hoped to be out of the building and avoid contact with him ever again. Angrily she reached for the car door, but her hand stopped. All the windows in the office were dark. *Where in the hell is he?*

When she stepped out of the car the wind whipped at her, blowing dust and bits of paper around. Lightning flashed on the distant horizon, followed by thunder rumbling faintly. Kasey ducked her head and shielded her eyes from the flying debris. She put her key in the lock and then realized the door was ajar. She opened it slowly.

Kasey quickly reached around and switched on the office lights before she entered the building. She stood there amazed and shaken. The room was in chaos. Papers were strewn about and furniture toppled. Had Forbes done this? Where was he?

"Forbes! Josh! Victor!"

No answer. Picking her way through the mess, Kasey laid her keys and her purse on the desk. She noticed that the door into the warehouse was slightly open and she started towards it. Lightning flashed again, this time closer, and it briefly lit the interior of the room with an eerie glow.

A small, high window was the only natural light source in the warehouse but storm clouds prevented sunlight from shining through. It was difficult for her to see into the room. The shapes of two large crates and a small one could barely be seen in the center of the large area. In busier times the room would be filled with boxes.

A scraping sound came from the darkened room.

"Hello, who's there? Josh? Victor? Forbes?"

Back in Blanchard's office, his clerical assistant brought in a folder. He thumbed through it and pulled out a photograph.

Cort looked and then gestured at the image, "It's him."

"He was released from Leavenworth about a year ago — just in time to do a lot of damage," Blanchard noted, reading the information at the bottom of the page.

Cort grabbed the phone.

Kasey reached for the light switch to the warehouse and flipped it up. She stood in the doorway and looked around the room. Click! The lights went out. She reached over and felt for the switch, flicking it several times. "Damn storm has knocked out the power," she mumbled, backing into the darkened office. She fumbled in drawers searching for a flashlight. When she finally found one she grabbed it and moved back toward the warehouse.

A shrill ring from the telephone penetrated the silence startling Kasey again. Her hand flew to her mouth, stifling the gasp before it became a full-blown scream. *This is nonsense. The scraping noise was probably just the wind blowing something against the building.*

Kasey exhaled, realizing she had been holding her breath. She felt her way around the desk where the phone was still ringing. Picking up the instrument, she pressed the button down to connect the call.

"Come on, damn it, answer the phone, Kasey," Cort pleaded.

"Cimmaron Air."

"Kasey, thank God I reached you. Are you all right?"

"Cort? "

"Kasey, I want you to get out of there immediately." The urgency in Cort's voice unnerved her. Was the storm going to be worse than first predicted and how would Cort know about it in Oregon?"

"What's wrong? Where are you?"

"I'm here in town. No more questions, Kasey, just get out of there and—"

Click.

"Cort, Cort, are you there?" The line was dead. She hung up and glanced out the window. Lights were on across the runway and she stood wondering how that could be, when a noise behind her made Kasey turn around. Immediately she heard the *whoosh* of an object slicing through the air and a sharp pain exploded against the side of her head. She saw pinpoints of bright lights just before she sank into a dark, enveloping void.

Kasey fought against the blackness. There was something she needed to do but she couldn't remember what it was. Someone grabbed her under her arms, lifting her up, and dragged her across the floor. She lay where the intruder dropped her. She could hear sounds like faint explosions and Kasey wondered what he was doing. When she tried to move, fingers of pain clawed through her head. *If I lie still for a minute —wait, someone is moving around me. Forbes?*

Cort slammed the phone down and turned to Blanchard, panic on his face. "Someone cut the line. We've got to get over there."

"How do you know that? It could be the storm."

"I just know, all right?"

"You and Frank will stay right here, Navarro." Blanchard made a quick phone call. He then walked swiftly through the police station, followed by Cort and Frank.

"Look, Lieutenant, either I go with you or I'll be put in jail for reckless driving."

Blanchard stopped at his commander's office, knocked and walked in.

"You'll play hell leaving me here, and don't give me that bull shit about the liabilities of a civilian riding with you. I take full responsibility," Cort called after him.

Blanchard nodded hesitantly, giving the report to his commanding officer. "Yes, sir. I'm on my way. You'll give me the info when you get it?"

Chapter Fifteen

Kasey heard footsteps and heavy breathing. *Someone is here with me. He's close, whoever it is. What happened? Where am I? Darkness. Ah, now it's starting to come back. The lights went out and someone hit me, probably the person I hear moving around. Forbes' car was outside and he had made threats in the past. Is he carrying them out now? Who else would want to harm me? Must lie still and wait for a chance to escape.*

Her vision slowly returning, Kasey could barely make out a man's outline. He seemed to be looking for something. Walking into the office, he pulled the warehouse door closed behind him and then walked outside. *Forbes was probably outside earlier when I heard that noise instead of in the warehouse. The sound had just seemed to come from inside the room.*

Then she heard the click of a switch being thrown and lights glowed around the crack in the door. Evidently she had left the warehouse light switch off when she kept flipping it. She crawled behind one of the larger crates and hoped the man would think she was still unconscious.

The storm had moved closer and lighting streaked across the sky, lighting the room just as he came back. Kasey was momentarily blinded by the sudden intrusion of light and he stood in silhouette, making it impossible to see his face. She hunkered down, waiting until her eyes readjusted to the darkness.

He stood in the doorway. "Kasey, come on out."

"Oh, Victor, am I glad to see you!" Kasey cried. She stumbled as she stood up and made her way to him. "Forbes hit me over the head and I thought you were him coming back to finish the job."

"Actually, I am — not Forbes—here to finish the job I started." He reached over and switched on the lights. "Forbes had a little accident. He won't be bothering you anymore. In fact, you won't be around to bother." He threw back his head and she heard chilling laughter. The sound was maniacal.

"What? Why?"

"Let's just say, settling an old debt."

"I don't understand, Victor."

"It's not important now. Besides I have work to do and there's little time." Victor moved toward her with a rope in his hand. "I'm afraid you're about to commit suicide and I'm the unfortunate person who finds you and calls the police."

Kasey took steps backwards, away from Victor. "You bastard! You're the one responsible for all the accidents." The realization left Kasey shaking with anger. "You tampered with my plane. When that failed to kill me, why didn't you finish the job? There were plenty of opportunities."

"I had other plans. After I got your father out of the way I wanted to destroy his reputation and I wanted to drive the business under, then there would be reason for you to commit suicide and no one would question it. The major 'accidents' had to look like just that."

"You're Richards! Why did you kill Pop? Revenge? And what have I done? I don't even remember anything about my past. I only found out when I read the newspaper accounts today."

Kasey backed up again and put a little more distance between herself and Victor. Sweat began to trickle down between her breasts. Fear, stark and vivid, twisted around her heart. She needed to stay calm, or at least give the appearance that she was, and come up with a plan. Otherwise, she was soon going to be Victor's next victim. *Must keep him talking.* "What were you looking for when you tore up the office?"

"I was looking to make sure your father didn't have more things hidden here for folks to find. And the missing money would be a nice little bonus." He stepped on his injured foot and winced. When he started walking again, his limp was even more pronounced. Angrily, he turned back to her.

"Thanks to him, I broke my ankle when I jumped out of the plane and I damned near flew into the mountain with him. If he had recognized me earlier, I would've gotten out sooner and landed on target."

"I should have put two and two together when you gave me that story about flagging for him, but I wasn't thinking clearly. I don't recall my Pop ever having a crop dusting job in New Mexico, now that I look back. And how did you get here from Colorado so quickly?"

Victor pushed a carton under one of the exposed beams overhead and Kasey kept moving slowly, making her way closer to the door. "Now that was ingenious of me. I arranged to fly here on a cargo plane. When we touched down I just walked across the tarmac when I saw your lights still on."

"Did you kill McNamara?"

"Greedy bastard. After he found Patrick he pulled a fast one and disappeared. I had paid him half up front and he didn't stick around for the *final pay off*. The last laugh was on him, though. I found my old pal with the info McNamara did provide to me." Victor laughed sardonically. "As luck would have it I found his message to you and took care of him. Unfortunately, I hightailed it out of here in such a hurry I forgot to erase the message. A situation I took care of later. Stop moving, Kasey." He closed the distance between them, gripping her arm and then looped the rope over her head, pulling the knot securely.

Red lights flashed on the police cruiser as Blanchard sped through the streets, dodging any cars that didn't pull over. His one concession to Cort's demand was allowing him to tag along, but Frank had to stay at headquarters. Putting one life at risk was bad enough; he wasn't going to make it two.

"According to the *Akron Beacon Journal* Richards had Mrs. O'Brien and five-year-old Kasey in the basement of an old deserted house beside a river."

"So how did they find O'Brien's family?" Blanchard's eyes moved from the traffic to Cort and back again.

"I'm getting to that. Richards told O'Brien to keep his mouth shut and to leave town, or he would never see his family again. Once O'Brien was out of the way, Richards said he would send his family to him, but actually he planned O'Brien's murder. Richard's knew O'Brien would spill his guts once Fran and Kasey were reunited with him.

"He didn't think his plan through very well because everything started falling apart around him. The cheap hood he hired to do away with O'Brien wanted more money and Richards was paranoid about someone finding his victims before his plan was completed, so he had to keep checking on them. That turned out to be his downfall."

"Unreal. Sounds like the plot for a low budget movie," Blanchard said.

"O'Brien left, but he didn't go far. He dogged Richards' footsteps day and night. It only took three days. Finally, on one of Richards' visits to the cabin Patrick was behind him. When Richards left that day O'Brien tore the place apart and found his family in the basement."

"Lieutenant, we checked with the phone company about the area you requested." A female voice came over the car radio. "No service has been interrupted."

Blanchard picked up the mike. "Thank you."

A shadow of alarm touched Cort's face and his brows drew together in an agonized expression. "Can't you make this thing go any faster?"

"We're almost there. Did this man, Richards, kill the wife?"

"There had been severe thunderstorms and rain for several days. The river overran its banks and the place was partially flooded when O'Brien found them. Kasey was huddled in a corner on an old sofa. She was in pretty bad shape. Her mother was even worse off. She had been beaten and had developed pneumonia, which eventually killed her. Kasey was in therapy for a while, then she and her father left the state. They moved around a lot before settling here."

"How do you know all of this?"

"Expensive detective and a lot research. The detective found the hood Richards hired and the hood gave him some of the story. Most of the story, of course, was in the local newspaper accounts of the kidnapping and trial. It ran in the paper for weeks. The detective sent me copies from the newspaper archives along with transcripts of the trial. Also Frank connected some of the dots." Cort glanced at Blanchard. "I also started on this long before you did."

"Why? What made you start looking into this right away?"

"My half-brother was on Kasey's plane the time the engine was sabotaged as you *aptly* pointed out. I knew he had been involved with her company, but I didn't know how. Spence and I had to find out if he had anything to do with cutting the oil line, or if he was the target. Then we found he had loaned Patrick something like a hundred and fifty thousand dollars.

"Richards had this same detective working on finding the O'Briens' before he got out of prison. Someone you know."

"Red McNamara," Blanchard answered. He twisted the steering wheel violently and Cort swore at him. He ignored the remark.

"Yes. I'm not sure if McNamara developed a conscience and was going to warn Kasey, or if he thought he could get money out of her, too. I met with him a couple of times in Colorado. He wanted quite a lot of money, most for his trouble and the balance for this hood. I did a little bargaining, but his price was still high. I had to round up the money or I would've had the story a lot sooner. Whatever his motive, it ended his life. "

"After McNamara found O'Brien, he also blackmailed him, probably to keep his whereabouts secret. I guess that didn't last long, because O'Brien was killed either by McNamara or Richards," Blanchard stated. "Here we are."

The police cruiser screeched to a halt in front of Cimmaron Air and both men jumped out, running toward the office door. Blanchard pulled his service revolver from under his jacket and pushed Cort behind him. They burst through the door, heads turning in both directions as they ran.

"Kasey! Kasey!" Blanchard waved his revolver toward the hangar door and then proceeded to check it out.

Victor held Kasey with her back against his chest, his arm clenched across her throat. He had dropped the opposite end of the rope that was fastened around her neck. In his other hand he held a gun pointed at the door. She lifted a foot and scraped her heel down his shin as hard as she could, then stomped on his injured ankle. He immediately released her and hopped around on the other leg. Kasey struggled with Victor, and he dropped his gun. She swung a closed fist and connected with his jaw, then she punched him in the stomach. He went down, but managed to crawl over and pick up the weapon, aiming it at her.

 Scuffling sounds of the fight came from the warehouse and both Cort and Blanchard bolted through the door at practically the same time. Victor was still on the floor, his breath slowly returning. Kasey drew her foot back to kick him in the face and his head snapped around as the two men burst through the door.

"Drop it! Now!" Blanchard ordered, aiming his weapon at Victor.

Victor blinked and turned the gun toward the lieutenant. Blanchard gave Cort a push out of harm's way and fired at Victor's hand.

"He killed my Pop!" Kasey cried, collapsing into Cort's arms and he gently lifted the noose over her head.

"And McNamara and a waitress in Colorado."

"He killed Forbes, too, but I don't know what he did with the body." Kasey threw her hands over her face. "I took him in. I trusted him."

Forbes' body had been discovered in the hangar and removed. Victor's hand was bandaged and he was placed in the police cruiser. Lieutenant Blanchard then got behind the wheel and waved as he drove away from the building.

Cort handed Kasey a copy of Red McNamara's report. The original was held at the police station as evidence.

"So that's why I'm afraid of storms," Kasey acknowledged, reading McNamara's report and recalling the newspaper accounts she found earlier.

"It makes sense to me, but I'm no psychologist."

"The report explains a lot. Victor had access to almost every part of my life. Having been a pilot, he knew how to wreck my plane and slipping the note under my door would have been easy enough. He also had the opportunity to break the ladder and make it look like an accident. Later, he shot himself in the leg to make it look like he was a victim as well.

"He found the message on my voice mail from Mr. McNamara and erased it. I thought I had done it. That's why it wasn't there when I went back to check for Lieutenant Blanchard. Not only that, he assumed — correctly, I might add —that I had found the clippings about the kidnapping and when I left he looked to see if there was anything more. That's why the office was so torn up."

"By the way, why do you call your father's friend Lieutenant Blanchard? Why so formal?"

"Because that's what I've called him since I was little. My father never allowed me to call grown-ups by their first names. It got to be a habit, besides, he *is* Lieutenant Blanchard."

"Do you remember anything about that time in your life?"

"No, I don't remember anything except being in the basement with water all around and a man wading through it towards me. When I recalled the scene I felt terrified of him but I didn't know why. I didn't even remember being in the basement until just recently when I saw the news clippings. I think it started to come back when we were at the line shack. The smell and the rain— I've heard of people blocking out part of their life but I don't understand it. How can you not remember something that would be so—well, for want of a better word— memorable?"

Kasey shifted in her seat. "Now that we've got my mystery cleared up, I need to know why all the secrecy about your heritage."

"First, I wanted my father to acknowledge me. Then because Neal's rejects thought I would be the next big catch. A couple of them found out and tried to make him jealous by putting the moves on me."

"And the trips?"

"In the beginning I thought maybe Neal was the target when your plane was sabotaged. I hired a private detective to find out what he could about your background. I already knew about Neal's and most of the enemies he had made. When you told me about your father, I had to find out just who was the target and why." Cort shrugged matter-of-factly. "A few of the trips were to see our attorney. I'm buying Neal's share of the ranch and working on getting Raymond's share."

Kasey studied his face for a beat. "Your father?" Cort clenched his mouth tighter and looked way.

Kasey finished packing the contents of her bedroom. She picked up the old photo taken with her father, wiping the face of it with her hand. She gazed at it for a minute recalling those happier times and smiled. At least she could smile now. Happiness would come back eventually. As she reached for the tissue paper to wrap it securely before putting it in the carton with the other photos and keepsakes, the photo slipped from her hand and fell to the floor, its frame breaking apart.

"Damn it." Kasey began picking up the pieces of glass and tossed them in the small box she had put aside for trash. She picked up the photo with its cardboard backing and found that there was something wedged between the two. She separated them and found a key and what appeared to be a letter taped to the cardboard.

Opening the envelope Kasey hastily pulled out the folded paper inside.

Dear Kasey,

If you have this letter in hand, it's not a good sign for me. I have received word that an old enemy has tracked me down who wants nothing better than to see me dead and since you are reading this it probably means he has succeeded.

You always teased me about moving around so much and that is why. But one can never confuse a bloodhound.

Anyway, you have probably noticed the key by now. It fits a locker in the airport terminal across the way from Cimmaron Air. I have a rental agreement for it. The locker number is on the key. In the locker you will find some cash I had stashed for a get-away (a lot of good that will do me now). No, I'm not being ghoulish, it's just that had I managed to come through the "reunion" to tell about it, this letter would have been destroyed and I would be using the money to celebrate.

I take it that since you are in possession of this letter, you have managed to slip through his murderous hands. So, my darling daughter, consider the money your dowry. I know, I know, that term no longer exists.

Take care and always remember I love you so very much. Take comfort in the fact that your mother's wait is over, because by this time I will be with her. So, until such time as you join us (which I hope is a very, very long time) I bid you a heartfelt goodbye, with all my love.

Pop

Kasey choked back the sobs. If she had been able, she would've laughed at the irony of it. But then, eighty thousand dollars wouldn't have saved the business and she sure as hell wouldn't have turned it over to Neal. Now that the case was settled she wouldn't have to either. She could certainly use a "leg up" on her new life, whatever that might be. In a small way that thought was invigorating.

Looking around the apartment, Kasey had to admit she didn't own too much more than her father, relatively speaking. Perhaps that was a good thing. She stood in the middle of the room amidst the crates and boxes with tears still running down her face, her sorrow a huge, painful knot inside. The transfer company would be here soon and take everything to storage until she settled in a permanent place.

The intercom buzzer broke the silence at the same time the phone rang and startled Kasey. She rubbed her arms briskly, erasing the goose flesh and she pressed the button to release the door downstairs.

"Come on up. The door's open." Kasey picked up the phone. "Hello."

"How's my Lady Ace?"

"Spence? Are you in town?"

"No, sorry, but I have a proposition for you."

"Why, you sly old dog."

Spence's voice held a trace of laughter. "Now, girl, don't make me forget why I called you. The ranchers around here have decided to hire you to fly for them. It's a beginning. Maybe you can build a business up here."

"I don't have a plane." Kasey looked at the key lying beside her purse. "At least not yet."

"Well, Cort is on his way to pick you up for the trip to Mexico. We'll discuss things when you get back."

Chapter Sixteen

Cort picked up the suitcases from the tarmac and started toward the terminal doorway. Consuelo and Kasey hurried to keep up with him. This trip to Mexico had come at an inconvenient time but he had made plans earlier and knew if he didn't make the trip now, he probably never would.

"Are you sure you are ready for this, *mi angelito*?" Consuelo asked, using the name she called him only in private. "I don't like these people for what they did to you and your mama. They are not nice people."

"It'll be okay, Consuelo. What more can they do? Tell us to leave? This is something I must do. Once and for all I need to confront my heritage."

"But it is also in America, *verdad*? Couldn't you just be happy with that? I don't want to see you hurt."

Cort set the luggage down as they neared the customs desk and reached inside his jacket pocket for their passports. He handed Kasey and Consuelo theirs, then smiled and affectionately patted Consuelo's shoulder. "It'll be all right, I promise," he repeated.

From the front seat, Cort stared out the window with mixed emotions as the taxi wound around the curves. His stomach knotted and his heart beat quicker. There was something else he could not identify. Was it sadness being so close to his mother's home, where she had lived and died? It was here she had been real and not just a painting on the wall. Her grave was in this town, but as Consuelo had angrily pointed out, it was not in his family's plot.

Cort's body was tense and the stress in his face and eyes were heart- breaking when he glanced over his shoulder at Kasey. She sat forward and reached over the seat, draping her arms over him. Pressing her lips against his neck, she gave him a kiss and smiled lovingly at him. His faint smile in return held a touch of sadness.

Kasey's heart ached to see him like this; she was so used to his strength and self-assurance. She had been uncertain about making the trip with him. She felt it was something he needed to do for himself, but couldn't refuse when she saw how much Cort wanted her to accompany him.

She had hoped Cort would propose to her before the trip and they would spend their honeymoon in Mexico, but that didn't happen. Perhaps he had too much on his mind, or was so stressed over meeting his family. This was a big step toward establishing his heritage and that meant so much to him.

Kasey turned and looked out the window of the cab. Large and small houses dotted the hillsides. Numerous at first, the dwellings were now fewer, and further apart. She assumed they would soon be coming into an area where the large estancias were located, that of Cort's grandparents among them. The road curved, revealing still another small community.

Suddenly Consuelo leaned forward and asked the driver to stop. She opened the door and stepped outside the cab, staring at a whitewashed, bougainvillea-covered cottage across the street. Tears brimmed her eyes and she angrily wiped them away.

"What's wrong, Consuelo?" Cort asked, following her gaze. "Is that your family home? We can stop in for a visit if you like."

"No, I did not know my family. This is where you were born and where your mother died." This time the tears slowly found their way down her cheeks as she crossed herself. "I tried to get help for her but I was too late." Consuelo hung her head and stood for a moment. "If only her family hadn't denied her."

Cort stepped from the vehicle and stood beside Consuelo. He looked up and down the street, taking in the neighborhood. He offered a hand to Kasey but she indicated she would wait in the cab.

Putting his arm around Consuelo, he held her close. "You did all you could do, my friend. No one could've done more and I am grateful to you. You loved my mother very much, didn't you?"

"She was mi *angelita*, like my own *hija*. She had no one else, *pobrecita*, *pobrecita*," Consuelo cried and wrung her hands.

"Are you sure this is the place? It's been more than thirty years," Cort asked, glancing across the street. He still held Consuelo close to his side.

"*Si*, I'm sure. We lived here for six months. Her papà, *cabron viejo*, didn't want her around when he found out and her waist began to thicken. I know this town for many years. This is the house."

Cort stood looking at the cottage for a moment then started across the street.

"What are you doing, *M'jito*?"

"I'm going to ask the family if we might come in."

"*Por que*?"

"I want to see where my mother spent her last days." Cort walked up to the door and knocked softly. When there was no answer he knocked harder.

"There is no one there," a young boy informed them in Spanish. He leaned against the doorframe of his nearby house and watched the strangers curiously.

"Who lives here, *Niño*?" Cort asked, squinting as he looked into the sun.

"No one, *Señor*. It has been empty for a month now."

Kasey climbed outside the cab and stretched her legs while Cort checked out the house. She was torn between going with him in support, or giving him privacy in his quest. It would no doubt be emotional, as was this journey so far. Since he didn't ask her to join him, she stayed by the taxi.

Cort walked around the side, checking windows to see if any would open. He peered inside and saw that the house was indeed empty. Finally he tried the doors until one opened, creaking against the intrusion.

The interior was dark and cool, a respite from the glaring noonday sun.

The floors were littered with trash discarded by the former tenants, but the house itself was in good condition, considering its age. The kitchen in back where Cort entered was small, with only moderate cabinet and counter space. He glanced over his shoulder into the back yard and saw an earthen oven where summer cooking was done to keep from heating the house.

Walking through a door into the rest of the dwelling, he entered a long narrow room, probably the dining room given its proximity to the kitchen. From there he traveled toward a large front room with a door to one side. That door led to a hallway, down which were two small bedrooms and a bathroom. The bathroom appeared to have been updated through the years.

Cort stood in the doorway of the larger bedroom for a time until Consuelo came up behind him and took his arm. "Come, *M'ijo*, we should be leaving now, we have a way to go yet." Hesitantly, Cort turned and headed for the front door, wiping at a tear that escaped and trailed down his cheek.

He stared out the taxi window for a time, until he finally said to Kasey, "I felt such a sadness in that room, and for many reasons. She was so young and so beautiful with a long life ahead of her and she never had a chance to fulfill it. I think too, because she suffered so. The main reason, though, is because I never got the chance to know her. I'm so glad she had Consuelo."

Cort was silent the rest of the trip. Pensively, he watched the countryside slip by while his stomach churned with apprehension. Maybe Consuelo was right and he shouldn't have come. Maybe he should have left well enough alone. He was about to tell Consuelo he had changed his mind when she announced they were entering the ranch's boundaries.

"We'll be at the gate soon, *M'ijo.* Just relax and be yourself," she said, patting him on the shoulder.

"I will wait for you in the car," Kasey said.

"You'll do no such thing. You and Consuelo are coming in with me. I won't accept 'no' for an answer this time." Cort leaned forward, looking up at the sky. Threatening clouds were building in the south. "I need you both for support. Besides, with the look of those clouds we won't stay long."

The trip was to be a short one and to the point. A journey that wouldn't have been possible if Cort's grandfather Navarro was still alive. Cort had questions and he was curious about the family he'd never met. If all went well this trip, he might return another time.

As they drove onto the yard, the door opened and an elderly woman stepped out. She was dressed in black slacks and blouse. A few dark strands streaked through her silver hair, which was pulled back from a center part and twisted into a knot at the back of her head. She ran a hand along her head smoothing the hair above an ear, the only indication that she, too, was nervous over the meeting. It was easy to see where his mother had gotten her beauty. Had his mother lived, perhaps she would've been the image of the woman standing on the porch.

"That is your *abuelita*, your grandmama," Consuelo whispered. "It has been a long time, but I would recognize her anywhere."

Cort stepped from the automobile and helped Kasey out. While she and Consuelo waited by the cab, he covered the distance to the porch quickly. He extended his hand to his grandmother. "*Buenos tardes, Señora.*"

Señora Navarro stepped forward and took his hand, her chin quivering, tears welling in her eyes. For a moment she could not speak, her gaze sweeping slowly over Cort.

"You look like your grandfather when he was your age," she breathed, barely above a whisper. Her glance took in the two women by the cab and she motioned for them to join her. Though agile for her seventy years, her movements were awkward as she dropped Cort's hand and turned toward them.

"Won't you come inside? Jorge will bring us something cool to drink. I'm sure you all must be tired and thirsty after your trip." She motioned to her son and turned back to her guests, "We will bring in your luggage and you can freshen up."

"We are registered at a hotel in the city. I didn't want to impose on your hospitality, besides our trip will be a short one. I have important business back in the States. And I wasn't sure —" he cleared his throat. "You remember Consuelo?" He tried to keep the bitterness from his voice. "And this is my friend, Kasey."

Señora Navarro took each woman by the hand, "Consuelo, I owe you so much I can never repay and I hope you will forgive me." She turned to Kasey. "*Con mucho gusto*. I see my grand—Cort has good taste in friends. You are lovely, my dear. I'm Arianna. You are welcome in my house."

Tears filled Arianna's eyes and spilled down her cheeks. Cort pulled a handkerchief from his pocket and handed it to her. "I am so sorry for everything. Your grandfather was a proud man, sometimes too much so. He was hurt terribly and felt betrayed by the man — your father, who was a guest in our home. I'm afraid he was too thickheaded to forgive and he forbade me to 'interfere'. His words, not mine."

"My mother died because of him. How could he just turn his back when she needed him and you the most? I don't know if I can ever understand or forgive that." Cort's voice choked with sorrow and anger and Kasey moved forward, putting her arm around his waist.

"You have to understand our culture." The elderly widow dropped her head in her hands and sobbed. "You don't know how I have suffered because of that. I didn't find out until later that she had — I would have gone to her." She turned her head away and looked out over the land. "As it is, I lost a daughter and a grandson."

"She made me promise not to get in touch with any of you," Consuelo interjected. "I didn't want to add to her distress, so I promised I wouldn't. And I was too busy trying to get help for her."

Cort went to his grandmother. "I didn't mean to upset you, *Señora* Navarro, It's just that I have carried this anger for so long and was not allowed to confront the Señor Navarro with it."

"Can you not call me Grandmama?"

"Maybe, one day," he answered.

Epilogue

Kasey shifted in the saddle then reached down and patted her horse. She was happy to be back at the ranch where it was peaceful and quiet. The past two weeks had been a flurry of activity with the storage of her things, Victor's arrest and arraignment, the trip to Mexico, now her second trip to Briar meadows. Any other events or matters would just have to wait. She was going to thoroughly enjoy this visit.

"So what's the surprise?" Kasey asked.

"You'll see. It's just a little farther and I think it's time to bring out the blindfold." Cort pulled a red bandana from his pocket and then urged his horse next to hers. Leaning over he tied the bandana around her head and picked up her horse's reins.

"Can you see anything?"

"Nope, not a thing."

"Good. No fair peeking. You'll spoil the whole effect."

"Is it the beaver pond? Are there new little beavers?"

"You'll see very soon."

"Boy, you sure know how to show a girl a good time!" Kasey laughed, grasping the saddle horn.

Cort's mouth curved with tenderness. It had been a long time since he last heard her laugh. He led her horse over a small rise and stopped, then leaning over he removed the kerchief. When Kasey looked at him, he pointed in the opposite direction.

There stood the line shack where Kasey had fainted. It had been painted white and a new porch graced the front of the cabin; plants hung in snowy wicker baskets from the beams. She jumped off the horse and ran toward the cabin, where two white, high-backed rockers with red cushions sat side-by-side on the porch. Kasey sat down in one, rocking slowly back and forth and running her hands along the arms. She turned to Cort, her smile eager and alive with affection and delight.

"You remembered."

Cort nodded. "This is your retreat. When you're not flying for Spence and you feel the need for space, you can come here. Of course, I'll join you once in a while." He nodded at the two matching rockers. "At least you can have some privacy, because the cowhands wouldn't be caught dead in a girlie place," he added. "We also installed a couple of windows and a skylight so it won't be dark inside."

Cort reached his arms above his head, as though stretching, and grabbed for the beam, smiling down at her. Abruptly he straightened and brought one arm back down, holding something in his hand. "Wonder what this is?"

Kasey looked up, her lips forming an unconscious smile. "What is it?"

"Must be something left here by the carpenters."

"Well, open it and see what it is." Kasey said, leaning forward in the rocker.

"Why don't *you* open it?" With a slow, secret smile he handed Kasey an old tin box, the label painted during another century. The lettering was almost obliterated and the colors muted.

Kasey turned the box over and over, trying to make out the message. Something bumped around inside. Hoping the product was still in there from that earlier time, she eagerly pulled at the box top, but it didn't budge. She looked up at Cort.

"Try harder. I think I saw it give a little."

"I'm trying." She tugged harder. Suddenly a thought occurred to her. "It's my personal key to the door, isn't it? You put the key in here." She tugged harder still. At once the lid came off and a square black velvet box fell into her lap. She stared, tongue-tied.

"Well, open it."

"I can't. My hands are shaking too much."

Cort took the box from her, opened it and removed the object it held. He reached for her hand and slipped a raised solitaire diamond set in a gold band on the appropriate finger. "You will marry me, won't you? I mean, I think it's bad luck to take the ring off again."

Kasey stood up. On tiptoes she put her arms around Cort's neck and whispered in his ear, "Convince me."

"Lady Ace, you sure can be frustrating at times." He scooped her up and pushed the door open, hesitating before entering. "You're not going to faint on me, are you?"

"It depends on what you do and how you do it." She nuzzled his ear then burying her face in his neck, she breathed a kiss there.

"Nothing like pressure —" His next words were smothered by her lips.

end

Special Bonus Feature

SUMMER SKIES

A short story

Summer Skies

April Montgomery ambled back down the country road towards the rented farmhouse in no particular hurry. She was enjoying the warmth of the early summer sun and the scents and sounds that filled the air. Birds called to one another across the meadow, while katydids hummed non-stop. A myriad of wild flowers lent color and fragrance to the fields on either side of her.

Winter had been long and hard, spilling over into the springtime. April had been confined to the city for what seemed ages—confined by both the weather and work-related issues. The last two months she had fought for her job with a lifestyles magazine and for her integrity. The battle had left her physically and emotionally drained.

Over a year ago April had spent six months researching and writing a series of articles for which she had won several awards. In the midst of all the formal recognition, a co-worker accused her of plagiarizing his work. A long and tedious court battle ensued. She was ultimately declared innocent, but the damage had been done. Now she took comfort in this freedom.

A sudden puff of wind lifted the blond hair from her shoulders and twirled it about. At that instant, a shiver seized her body. April stopped for a moment. She had heard a sound accompanying the wind—a cry or moan, she couldn't tell which.

April strained her ears trying to hear it again. There it was— a faint anguished cry. It seemed to come from the large pin oak tree at the beginning of the wooded area a short distance from the road. The grasses were taller there and she could not see if someone in distress was under the tree.

Cautiously April crossed the ditch and headed toward the trees. Still she couldn't see anyone. She stood a moment and listened, then moved deeper into the woods. The air was cool and scented by an earthy dampness. A small stream trickled nearby and something scurried into the bushes.

"Hullo, anybody there?" She listened intently, but no answer came.

What should I do? Turning in a complete circle, April listened and watched for any movement. If someone was in trouble she didn't want to leave. On the other hand, what if someone was leading her into danger? In the past she wouldn't have given it much thought, but after all she had been through April was paranoid. Perhaps she should go get help.

April ran all the way to the farmhouse and dialed the sheriff's department. She hurriedly explained to an officer what had happened and asked if he would come out and search the woods.

"Miss Montgomery, do you think maybe it was just the wind blowing through the trees making that sound? You said you couldn't see anybody and no one answered when you called out."

"I'm pretty sure I heard someone moan, Sheriff. If you don't want to come over here and check it out, I'll go back myself. What if someone is lying out there hurt and I just couldn't see them from where I was?" April's voice held a note of desperation.

"Now calm down. I didn't say I wouldn't come. I just wanted to cover all bases. You stay where you are and I'll send a couple of deputies out there. Give me directions to the spot where you thought you heard the voice."

"You know where the McNary farm is? Well, it's just before you get there coming from town. Tell the officers I'll be waiting alongside the road."

April disconnected the call and headed out the door to meet the deputies. She wanted to be sure their search was thorough and that there would be no question they gave it their best shot. Only then could she relax.

When the deputies arrived, April was waiting at the exact spot she had heard the sound. They split up, but stayed within earshot of each other. For the next hour they searched every inch of the woods. There was no one to be found.

"I know I heard something. We must have missed— "

"Miss Montgomery, there is no one here. You saw for yourself. Now, it's going to be dark soon so you'd best be getting home. We need to get back to work." The deputy touched his hat brim and waited for her to go ahead of him.

April hesitated, listening once more, but decided that the deputy was right. They had looked everywhere. She turned and walked back to the road, the two deputies right behind her.

Later that evening April prepared a large salad for dinner, piling big chunks of broiled chicken on top. She grabbed a sack of saltine crackers and a frosty glass of iced tea, placed them on a tray with her salad and went out onto the porch to eat.

The air was warm and still and heavy with the scent of honeysuckle. Occasionally a breeze stirred but it was short-lived. It seemed millions of stars were sprinkled across the black velvet sky; some even appeared to be blinking, much like the sprinkling of fireflies darting around the front yard.

A gingerbread trim delicately framed the front of the porch, while pots of varied flowers hung from hooks at intervals above the white railing. A swing hung from the ceiling at the far end, a cushion in patterned green canvas covering the seat.

A white wicker settee, chair, and table were grouped together closer to the front door.

On the other side of the door were a table and two chairs where April chose to have her dinner. She was glad she elected to eat on the beautiful wrap-around porch. It was more relaxing than eating indoors.

She struck a match, squinting against the sudden burst of light, and touched the flame to a citronella candle in the center of the table to keep the mosquitoes from ruining her evening.

Even though she felt the tension slipping from her body, April was still more than a little troubled by the earlier events. Was it just her imagination playing tricks on her? It had to be. They had searched every inch of the woods within hearing distance of the road and even farther. Perhaps her exhaustion had played a part in all this. Then, too, she was unaccustomed to the sounds of country living and maybe the sheriff was right, it was just the sound of the wind blowing through the trees.

The sharp shrill of the telephone broke into her reverie. She gathered her empty dishes and went into the kitchen.

"Hello."

No one was there. She replaced the phone and started to clean up the dishes when the phone rang again.

"Who is this?" she demanded.

"April?"

"Oh, sorry, Peter. There was another call before yours but no one was there. I thought someone was playing tricks." April switched the phone to her other ear. "How are you? How are things going at work?"

"Fine on both counts. I miss you. We all do. It doesn't sound like *you* are doing well, though. You're supposed to be relaxing and taking it easy out there in the sticks."

"I am, it just takes a while to unwind. I'll be fine." April started to tell him about her earlier adventure, but decided against it. "To what do I owe the pleasure of your call? I haven't been gone long enough for you to be checking on me."

"How would you like some company?"

"I don't think that would be a good idea right now. I really need some time to myself— "

"Well, be that way." His laugh sounded forced, "But if you need me to come out there and rescue you from some hayseed, you'll let me know won't you?"

"You'll be the first person I call. Goodnight, Peter."

April replaced the receiver slowly, smiling. Peter Miles was a nice enough guy. She had dated him for a couple of years, but somehow there just wasn't a spark to their comfortable relationship. There were no second thoughts when it came to her reporting, but April had difficulty making decisions affecting her personal life. She too often stayed within her comfort range. She envied people who were able to make changes without too much thought, people who were able to pick up stakes and move on.

Leaning against the wall, she began to wonder about her future. Was there a place in it for Peter? Would she continue to work for the magazine? Would people question any future articles she wrote?

The telephone rang again and she jumped. Goosebumps freckled her arms. She rubbed them vigorously before she lifted the receiver.

"Did you forget something?" April laughed, thinking it was Peter again. Once more there was only silence on the other end. "Who is this? What do you want?" The connection broke off with a click and a dial tone buzzed defiantly in her ear. April slammed the phone back on its hook and briefly stared at the instrument, daring it to ring again.

April finished washing the bowl and utensils from her dinner and looked around the kitchen making sure it was tidy. The kitchen was a large, old-fashioned one, matching the old farmhouse.

A tall window above the sink looked out onto the side yard where, during the daytime, the view of a well-manicured garden took away from the drudgery of washing dishes. The walls on either side of the window were a creamy yellow bead board.

The L-shaped counter topped with Formica, ran under glass-fronted cabinets and framed a 1940's model gas range. The lower doors of the cabinet were solid and the same color as the wall.

On the other side of the kitchen were a refrigerator and a walk-in pantry. In the middle of the room stood a real butcher block island for preparing food. A small square table and two chairs were tucked away in the corner.

April wiped her hands on a paper towel, tossing it into the open wastebasket by the door. She switched off the light and made sure everything was locked tightly before she climbed the stairs.

The first two nights she had fallen into a dreamless sleep, having worn herself out making the house habitable. There had been covers to take off the furniture, floors to be swept and mopped, fresh linens to be put on the beds and groceries to buy. The chores also kept her too busy to think much about the last few months.

But sleep did not come easy to April this third night. There were sounds she hadn't noticed before; night sounds of the country and its creatures. Floors creaked and for a minute, April thought it sounded like someone walking. Her heart hammered against her chest as she got up and slowly made her way through the house, carrying the broom she had used earlier to use now as a weapon if she needed one. After inspecting every room, she was satisfied it had been only the house settling and she was alone. She crawled back into the bed.

When April finally did fall asleep, it was a restless one. Disjointed dreams and visions she couldn't remember the next morning, left her unsettled. She felt tired and drained, definitely in need of coffee.

April padded down the stairs and into the kitchen. Dragging out the coffeemaker, she began measuring out the dark crystals into its basket. She reached over to plug it in, when the sound of someone entering the front door demanded her attention. After quietly opening a couple of drawers she found the knives and retrieved one. Holding it in front of her, she went to see who or what had entered her house uninvited.

"Oh, hello. I didn't know you had moved in yet." Seeing the large knife she gripped, he put his hands in the air.

"Who are you and how did you get in here?"

"Can you put the knife down?" He nodded toward the weapon she pointed at him.

"If you'll answer my question first."

"My name is Mark McNary. I own this house and I came to make sure everything was in order for your arrival. You were supposed to be here this afternoon, right?"

"Three days ago." April eyed him suspiciously, not lowering the knife.

"My apologies. I'll just go now and come back to see you at a more appropriate time." His glance swept her from head to toe, then came to rest on the knife.

April was suddenly aware she was still in her nightshirt. "If you'll just wait on the porch—I have coffee on." Only when he went out the door did she lower the knife. She carried it upstairs and hastily tugged on jeans and a tee shirt.

Mark was tall, at least six feet-two, and a handsome man with a muscular build. He had sandy brown hair and tawny eyes. He seemed quite comfortable leaning against the porch railing, watching the front door as April emerged.

"I apologize again for the intrusion. I truly thought you were getting here this afternoon." An easy smile played at the corners of his mouth. "How about joining me for dinner tonight and I'll make this up to you?"

"Apology accepted, but I have to decline the invitation. Thanks anyway." Something about this man didn't sit well with April. Until she knew him better, she would keep her distance.

"Well, I guess I won't keep you any longer. If you need anything, please feel free to call me." He fished in his pocket and withdrew a card, handing it to her as he left.

April stood on the porch and watched his car leave. As she turned to go back inside, she caught a glimpse of a pale young woman who had just slipped past the lilac bush in the front yard. At the corner, she turned and glanced forlornly at April, then disappeared behind the house.

"Hello! Who's there?" When there was no answer, April hurried down the steps and across the yard toward the back of the house. "Two visitors in one morning. So much for privacy."

No one was in the back yard. April stood a moment looking around, hoping the dark-haired woman might return if she waited long enough. Then again, she might have cut through the yard and gone into the woods, which bordered the property on three sides.

When no one materialized, April started to go back into the house, but noticed a shed at the edge of the yard. *Probably a tool shed. Maybe I can get in some gardening while I'm here. It's been a long time.*

The shed door stood ajar and April opened it cautiously in case a wild creature might be in there. The interior seemed dark after facing the bright morning sun, so she stood a moment until her eyes adjusted to the gloom. A cool, damp breath of air blew in her face and the fine hair on the back of her neck stood on end. For the second time goose bumps freckled her arms. She shut the door firmly, deciding gardening wasn't all that important after all.

"Good morning."

"Good morning," April answered, walking toward the elderly woman standing at the road's edge. *This place is busier than Grand Central Station.*

"I'm Gladys Rice, your neighbor. I see you met Mr. McNary." Gladys glanced down the road. "I'm not one to gossip much, but you need to look out for that one. He's like summer skies; nice and tranquil one minute and spewing forth violent storms the next."

"Thanks for the warning." April started up the steps, but Gladys stood there, giving no indication she had finished chatting. "Would you like to come up on the porch and have a cup of coffee with me?"

"Why, thank you, dear. I will sit a spell, but I've had my caffeine limit for the day."

"Well, I haven't had my coffee yet," April answered, a little more sharply than she had intended. "I have some lemonade in the fridge. How about a glass for you?"

"That will be fine, dear." Gladys didn't seem to notice the tone and she made herself comfortable in the wicker chair.

April smiled and hurried into the house. She poured a glass of lemonade for Gladys and a cup of coffee for herself, then sprinkled a fine layer of sugar-free sweetener on top.

"Thank you." Gladys sipped her drink and set the glass down on the table. "I hope you take good care of the flower gardens. Sara sure loves her gardens and would be unhappy if anything happened to them."

"Would that be Mark's mother?"

"Oh no, dear. She's Mark's wife."

"Where is she?"

"She went back east, couldn't put up with his temper. Such a sweet young thing and I'm glad she left him." Gladys took another sip of her drink. She studied April thoughtfully for a moment and stood up. "I guess I'll get going and let you get on with your day. "It's early and you've already had two visitors."

"Three," April corrected. "A young woman cut across my yard while ago. That's what I was doing in the back yard. Perhaps you know her—young—maybe in her twenties—with dark hair?"

"No, not anyone who lives around here. Sounds a little like Sara, but of course she's in—where was that Sara said she was going? It was New Jersey, New Hampshire, something like that."

"Are you sure she left?"

"She waved to me that morning as she backed her car out. I watched her until she was out of sight."

"Well, maybe this woman is visiting someone around these parts and I'll see her again." April shrugged.

Mrs. Rice turned to leave, but paused on the step. "I didn't catch your name."

"April, April Montgomery. Sorry for my bad manners but as you pointed out, it's early yet."

"Welcome to the neighborhood. I'll bring over a nice fresh pie for you once it cools." Gladys waved over her shoulder as she watched her steps carefully.

Late that afternoon, compelled by her curiosity, April took a walk toward the wooded area where she had last heard the spine-chilling sounds. It was now just about the same time of day, because the sun was low in the sky and the heat less intense.

As she neared the spot, April slowed her steps until she had completely stopped. She listened carefully. Nothing. The sheriff was probably right and she had imagined the sounds before. Disappointed, she turned back toward the old farmhouse.

The next few days April kept busy rearranging furniture and doing some light yard work that didn't require tools. She was still wary of the tool-shed. She decided to stay away from the "spot" in the woods, although curiosity almost got the better of her a couple of times. She didn't see the woman either, so April figured she had worked through her problem.

Glancing at her watch, she got up from her knees in the garden and brushed off her jeans. Her friend, Anna, was coming down from Dallas to have lunch. April had been gone a week and she suspected Anna's visit was to check on her and make sure she was all right.

April climbed the stairs and went to the bathroom, pushed the shower curtain aside and turned on the water. She leaned over and adjusted the knobs to the right temperature. While the tub filled, she went to the closet and pulled out a skirt and blouse, laying the clothes across the bed.

Pulling off her dirty clothes, April placed them in a small hamper in the closet, then padded into the bathroom. She closed the door behind her. Sticking one toe in the water to make sure the temperature was comfortable, she climbed in and slid down until she was submerged to her chin.

Suddenly she heard the floor creaking outside the bathroom. The door opened slowly and the hinges squeaked in protest. April's heart pounded. She jerked the shower curtain aside with false bravado. No one was there.

April stepped out of the tub, pulled a towel around her and ran out the door. She first looked down the hall towards the bedroom, then down the stairs. She leaned over the banister, but saw no one was below.

Running downstairs she checked the kitchen and the porch, then the living room. The front door stood ajar, but no one was on the porch or in the yard. April pushed the door shut and quickly locked it. She put the security chain on both front and back doors. If her landlord had used his key again to "check on things", she was going to give him a piece of her mind. She had been perfectly clear as to when she expected to arrive. Now, she wondered what had been his motive.

Suddenly the phone rang again and April's hand flew to her mouth, stifling the scream. Tears sprang to her eyes from fright. She picked up the phone and slowly put it to her ear. She listened for a moment, waiting for the person on the other end of the line to speak first.

When she heard a woman sobbing, she thought something had happened to Anna on her way down from Dallas. "Anna? Is that you? What's wrong?"

No answer. There was silence for a moment and then the click as the call was disconnected. April depressed the button and dialed star sixty-nine to see from where or whom the phone call had come. The phone number the automated voice gave her was Peter's and the day of the call was a few days earlier.

"But that's not possible! Who was on the phone just now?" She yelled into the phone. *If someone was trying to drive me out of my mind, it's working. Here I am shouting questions at a machine as though it would answer me.*

Still trembling from her fright, April climbed the stairs and returned to the bathroom. She listened for a time before getting back into the tub. Satisfied she was alone, she took the quickest bath ever.

Going into her bedroom, April found the clothes she had laid out on the bed tossed on the floor in a rumpled heap. Someone had definitely been in the house!

The wind had picked up and dark clouds scooted across the sky as April guided her car into the diagonal parking space. She deposited money in the meter then glanced in both directions as she hurried across the street toward the only upscale restaurant in town.

Anna was seated in the waiting area and jumped up when April entered, helping her pull the door shut against the strong wind.

"Wow. Did you arrange this for me?"

"Of course. Didn't want you to drive all the way here for just any old ordinary visit." April gave her friend a big hug, then held her at arm's length. "You've lost weight. New boyfriend?"

"I wish that was true, but I just plain got sick of my clothes being so tight and feeling tired all the time. I joined the gym and work out every day. What about you? I can't say this trip has been a restful one for you. You look awful."

"Thanks a lot, friend."

"Let's get a table. I want to hear what's been happening."

Anna listened intently as April filled her in on everything. Once or twice she bent closer when April mentioned her landlord and the fact that he walked in on her without knocking. "I think he may have come in while I was bathing today."

Anna raised an eyebrow and smiled.

"It's not like that. He—I don't know. There is something about him that raises the hackles, if you know what I mean."

"What about the young woman? Maybe she was the same who interrupted your bath. Seems to me she has been checking you out."

"I've only seen her that once. I'm not sure she has anything to do with the other things, though—the phone ringing and someone moaning in the woods. I've almost convinced myself the moaning part was my imagination, though." She swirled her straw around in the iced tea, watching it thoughtfully.

"What do you hear of Mason these days?" April tried to be casual when she asked about the man who had brought so much trouble into her life.

Anna's eyes widened. "Do you think he followed you down here?"

"I wouldn't put it past him. After all, he didn't take all that happened very well."

"And to whom does he owe that? Because he flipped out do you think he might be trying to drive you crazy? Wow. You might be right, too. I never thought about that." Anna stirred cream into her coffee. "Look, April, you be careful. I wish I could stay here with you—safety in numbers you know—but Howard has me set to fly to New Orleans tomorrow."

"What's in New Orleans?"

"Oh, it's just a convention he wants me to attend. You know how I *love* those things." Anna laughed and shook her head. "How much longer are you going to stay down here?"

"I'm not sure. I have the house for a month and by then, hopefully, I should be ready to re-join society." April sighed as she pushed the remains of her lunch around the plate with her fork. "I've been thinking—"

"Yes? Spit it out." Anna scooted closer to the table and propped her chin on her folded hands, waiting for April to continue. She knew by the tone in April's voice that what she was about to say would be a news flash.

"It's about Peter. I—I'm not sure I want to continue our relationship."

"That's quite the bombshell. Have you talked to him about this?"

"No, but I think he has a feeling, or maybe it's just my imagination. He called shortly after I got here and wanted to come down."

"And what did you say?"

"I told him I needed more time to myself." April placed her silverware across her plate and pushed it to one side. "I truly didn't want to see him and, for the first time, I started thinking about my life without him. You know something? It felt liberating."

"What do you think he'll do when you tell him? You *are* going to tell him?"

"Yes, now that I've made up my mind." April reached across the table and covered Anna's hand with hers. "I'm glad you came down here today. You've helped me make one decision I've been worrying about for some time."

"You mean you just came to that conclusion? Right this very minute? That's so unlike you—I mean, that's sudden for you."

"I know, but I think I've known inside for a while. I just needed to get away from him and to see everything in that part of my life clearly." April also had the decision to make about her future with the magazine, but that wasn't something she was ready to reveal just yet.

"Be careful, April. I don't like how things are going right now. Maybe you should put off talking to Peter until this other stuff is resolved. Otherwise you might have another man looking for revenge. Call me if you need me. I'll have my cell phone with me." Anna looked down at her watch. "My goodness, time flies when you're having fun. I need to get back to Dallas and pack for tomorrow. No telling what the weather is like out there for my drive home."

The sidewalks and streets were covered with a thin film of water and murky streams ran in the gutters. Droplets of rain still clung to the trees lining the street, but the dark clouds had been thinned and the wind had subsided.

April hugged Anna. "Be careful driving back. Give me a call when you get there so I'll know you made it home safely."

"Will do. Good luck with your quest. I'll be checking on your progress."

After she watched Anna's car disappear, April walked the block over to Mark's office. His receptionist informed her he had gone over to New Boston to see a client.

"How long has he been gone?"

"He left early this morning and said he wouldn't be back until three or four o'clock this afternoon."

April turned to leave. If Mark had been out of town, or so his employee said, there was no need to question if he had been the intruder in her house earlier. But who else had a key?

"Can I give him your name?"

"April. I rent his house."

As April pulled into the yard she saw the figure of the young woman walking towards the woods again. She turned and looked at April just before she disappeared among the trees. April got out of the car and ran after her.

"Hello!" There was no answer. Driven by a reporter's inquisitiveness, she followed the woman, catching only a glimpse of the green dress she wore. She stood a moment and listened carefully. Nothing. Then a moan rode the wind so low and distressed it caused chills to shiver up April's spine.

Was she going mad? Had anyone else heard this? Cautiously, she followed the sound. She took a few steps then waited—listening. This time she heard sobbing. It seemed to come from straight ahead. A few more steps and she saw the woman kneeling beneath a tree, rocking back and forth. When she looked up and saw April, she stood and took off deeper into the woods.

"Wait!" April called after her. "I just want to help you. Please come back." She turned around to get her bearings and noticed something familiar about the spot. There was the road where she had walked the first time she had heard that haunting cry. Well, the mystery was cleared up. At least she knew the sound had come from someone who was able to move about. Now she had to find out what was wrong and what the woman had been looking for.

Maybe she didn't want or need April's help. Perhaps she came out here to be alone. If that was true, though, why did it seem as though she wanted April to follow her?

April hurried toward the road. She needed to get to a phone and let the sheriff know she *had indeed* heard someone the day she had called. Maybe he could find out what was wrong. Surely the woman would trust a law officer. Would he know who she was?

The sound of a car engine caught April's attention. As she crossed the ditch and looked down the road, she recognized Mark McNary's approaching car. He stopped when he saw April and got out.

"Well, pretty lady, what are you doing out here? I was just coming to see you. My secretary said you were by the office earlier."

April explained about the young woman she had seen and that she seemed in distress. Also, she believed her to be the one she had heard crying previously.

"I want to let the sheriff know I wasn't crazy when I called him the other day."

"What did she look like? Maybe I know her."

"She's about my height, five-two. She has dark hair, fair skin and hauntingly dark eyes. She's wearing a green dress with a white collar."

Mark's face paled. "That's not possible."

"Do you know her?"

"You just described my wife. And the dress was the one she was wearing when she—she went away."

"Maybe she came back."

"I told you that's not possible." Mark's voice was cold and exact, evoking fear in April. "Where did you see her? Show me!"

When they reached the tree where the young woman had been kneeling, Mark walked around it several times, closely inspecting the ground.

"How did you know about this place?" His eyes narrowed suspiciously.

"I told you, I heard moaning—"

"Don't lie to me." He seized her quickly, his fingers digging cruelly into the flesh on her upper arm. "How did you know she was buried here?"

"Buried? Then she didn't go back east as people thought? What happened to her? How did she die?" April thought the question was inane, but she wanted to keep him talking until she could figure a means of escape. She had to reach safety and notify the authorities.

"Nobody leaves me unless I want them to. Especially my wife. She expected money for divorcing me." He released his hold on April and paced the site, keeping his eye on her. "How did you know so much about her? I want the truth this time. Are you a relative?"

"Your wife paid a visit to the house a few times and I followed her back here." April concealed her shock at the change in Mark.

"Don't get cute with me!" Mark struck her across the face.

April fell to the ground. For a minute she lay stunned, then put her hands out to push herself up. When she did, she grabbed a handful of dirt. She gripped the tree with her free hand for support and watched for the right moment. When Mark bent over to help her up, she reacted quickly. Tossing the dirt directly in his face, she ran as fast as she could through the woods towards the house.

The sound of thrashing bushes behind her told April she had succeeded in temporarily blinding Mark. Maybe she could get far enough ahead of him to call the sheriff once she reached the house.

Dark clouds skittered across the sky and the faint rumble of distant thunder indicated the previous storm was returning. Treetops swayed and the wind whistled through the woods. While April ran, her hair was whipped against her face and in her eyes, at times obstructing her vision.

Something whipped past April going in the opposite direction, but she hadn't seen what it was, only felt the cool breeze it generated. She dared not look back for fear Mark would be right behind her. Digging her heels in, she picked up speed and soon the house came into view.

April burst through the door and managed to lock it behind her. She reached for the phone with shaking fingers just as the shrill ring filled the kitchen, the sound heightened by her fear.

"Hello. April?"

"Oh, not now Peter, I have to make a call." April depressed the button and dialed 911. "Please Sheriff Owens, come out to the McNary place. He's going to kill me." She dropped the phone on the floor and looked around for something to block the door. She suddenly remembered: Mark had a key to the house!

Minutes later April heard the siren in the distance, but it stopped abruptly before it reached the house.

"No!" April ran out the door. All she could think of was getting to the sheriff and safety before Mark found her.

April slowed her step as she came upon the patrol car. The sheriff was bending over an object in the road. Maybe Mark had stumbled in front of the car and been hit.

"I think that's as close as you want to come," the sheriff cautioned. "Let me call my office and I'll be right there."

"Is he—"

"Tell me what happened here."

After April told the sheriff everything, including Sara McNary's murder, he scratched his head and looked toward the tree. "So you killed him in self defense?"

"Wha—no, I only threw dirt in his face. How—how did he die?"

"He had garden shears stuck in his gut when he ran out into the road. He died right here on the spot."

"I swear I didn't—where did the garden shears come from? Neither of us had anything like that—unless he went back to his car and got them. But that doesn't make sense."

*　　*　　*　　*　　*　　*　　*　　*

"It took a couple of weeks of investigation for us to unravel the mystery, but some of the story is still an educated guess." Sheriff Owens sat on the porch rolling the glass of cold lemonade between his hands.

"It seems, from tests we made, that Mark murdered Sara in the tool-shed and dragged or carried her into the woods where he buried her. I guess he figured no one would find her grave there. That's why you reacted as you did. I will never be able to figure that one out." The last comment he mumbled to himself.

"But Mrs. Rice saw her leave in her car. How did she get back here and where is her car?"

"The only two people who know the answer to that are dead." The sheriff took another sip of lemonade and held the cool glass to his cheek. "Anyway, he buried the shears with the body. They were probably just below the surface and when you threw dirt in his face, he must have fallen on them."

"Or maybe Sara returned the favor?" She grinned slowly at him.

Sheriff Owens took off his hat and scratched his head. "A couple of weeks ago I would have said you're as crazy as a loon, but now I guess anything is possible." He stared out into the yard for a minute, then asked, "I wonder if he knew she was pregnant?"

"O-o-o-h. That was the reason she was crying and the reason she wanted the truth to come out. One doesn't mess with a mother's child. How far along was she?"

"The coroner said about three months."

"How very sad." April shook her head slowly, trying to comprehend the tragedy.

"So, are you all packed and ready to go?" The sheriff changed the subject. "Will you be coming back this way sometime?"

"Probably not. I'm looking for a new job and new life. I don't know where that will take me, but now I'm ready for anything."

end